WYLDE WINGS

WYLDE WINGS

KATE RISTAU

Illustrated by
BRIAN W. PARKER

Cover design: Brian W. Parker

Interior design: Kate Ristau

Back cover design: Lee Moyer

Back cover photo: Rowan Ristau

Design support: Gigi Little

Sensitivity read: Viveca Shearin

For Rowan, who asked for the story of a boy with wings, and for Victor, who already has them.

Special thanks to Mrs. Anderson's English classes at Geneseo Middle School and Mrs. Stanfill's publishing class at Portland State University. This book shines because of all of you.
Write on, Wylde Ones!

PROLOGUE

THERE ONCE WAS A TOWN ON THE OTHER SIDE OF THE MOUNTAIN. It never did have a name, for it never needed one. The people there were happy, and life was easy. That little town was all they knew, and all they needed to know. They didn't dream higher than the mountain or swim far out to sea. They held their secrets close, and they kept their children in the light.

And for as long as they could remember, they flew.

Every twelve-year-old child, on the day they earned their name, was so filled with the spark that their wings would pop out, bursting through their fragile skin and into the morning light.

When the darkness came, and took their wings, they sent one small spark of light across the ocean. They hoped, they dreamed, that one day, the spark would return to them when they called.

Why stories are stupid

Mom loved stories. She told them all the time. Every night, every day, and for every situation, she had a

STORY.

First day of school? I remember...
Dog died? Let me tell you...
Can't find the salt? Years ago...
Mean friends? When I was little...

Even now, I can't look at the stars without remembering how the bear was lowered to the earth in a golden basket. I can barely enter a forest without thinking of the Wild Hunt. And, after all these years, I still can't stand seeing Christmas trees up past Twelfth Night. Don't they fear the Oak King?

Which is why stories are so stupid. Stories move you away from the everyday garbage of English class and physics lab and Mr. Wylde's obsession with **thermodynamics.**

Stories rescue you from Jules' endless prattling about Dr. Who (who?) and Jaiden's undying love of basketball statistics (three-pointers?). Stories offer

-->HOPE

And that's why they're so awful. They suck. They make you think that things will change. That people will be
   *Kinder
   *Smarter.
   *Not-dead.
But reality, well, that's a very different thing.

1

"The energy of an isolated system is constant," Mr. Wylde explained for the 800th time. "It doesn't change."

"And that's why we're headed to OMSI today," Mrs. Klein added in.

"We're going to see thermodynamics in action," Mr. Wylde continued. His eyes were glowing with excitement behind the giant plastic frames of his glasses, and the bright fluorescent light shined off his dark skin as he paced the front of the room.

I closed my notebook, crossed my arms, and laid my head down on my pile of books. This was going to take a while. He was clearly just getting started.

"There's research from eight of the founding schools of thermodynamics," Mr. Wylde said. "École, Glasgow, all the way through to the Dutch school. They even have Joseph Black's original notes on latent heat. It will be—"

"It will be mesmerizing," Klein said. "I'm sure. But you'll also see the new T-Rex, and the Dr. Who exhibit—"

"Yes!" Jules said, and the entire class laughed. She turned bright red and scooted deep into her seat, her red hair dangling in front of her face. She pulled out her pen, shifted her notebook with her prosthetic hand, and then she was gone. A forest of squares and blotted ink crossed the top of her notebook page.

I waved my hand at her, but she wouldn't look up from her desk. She gets so embarrassed, so worried about what people think. Who cares? They suck. And she's awesome.

I pushed up my glasses, opened my own notebook back up, and started to draw her a tiger. One of those anime ones. She'd like it. She was all worried for nothing – no one was paying attention to her anyway. Tapping fingers. Itching arms. Shaking legs. We were all ready to get out the door and onto the bus.

Especially me.

I can't stand science class. Mr. Wylde is so boring. I drew the large eyes of the tiger. He's always droning on about latent heat and thermodynamics. I sketched its giant teeth. We're in seventh grade! I shaded in its nose. We're not in college! I added pointy ears. We're supposed to be learning about volcanoes, geology, and worms. I gave the tiger huge paws. Instead, he's talking about energy – protons and neutrons. I crosshatched stripes across its flank. We never get to do anything cool and real like earth science or breeding fruit flies or dissecting frogs. I wrote *Hey Jules* on the top. It's all stuff that's not real and doesn't even matter.

He knocked on his desk to get our attention. "Don't forget to grab your lab notebooks!"

Ugh. This class is terrible and Mr' Wylde is so boring and dumb and...oh yeah...he's my dad.

I folded up the paper and passed it to Jules. She lifted her head, snatched the sheet, opened it up, and smiled. She tucked it into her pocket.

"Line up!" Mrs. Klein said.

"Yes!" Jules yelled. This time, she didn't blush. She shoved her notebook into her bag and jumped to her feet.

Jaiden pushed up the aisle and made his way over to us. He

was tying his long dark hair up on top of his head. "This is gonna be awesome. Do you think we'll get to ride the T-Rex?"

"Shut-up," Jules said. "They don't let you ride the—"

"It was a joke," Jaiden said.

"You're a joke," I said, knocking his hands away before he got the rubber band in.

"Burn!" Jules yelled.

Jaiden screamed like he was on fire, and started patting his hair. "*Fuego!*" he yelled. "It hurts! Put it out!"

"Shh," Mikka said. We ignored her, laughing and walking out the door toward the bus. It was going to be a good day. A GREAT day. I could feel it. Everybody was bouncing and skipping down the hall. We never get to go on field trips. Not at our school. Washington Middle is a school with a low-income population. That's a fancy term for a school full of poor kids. Half the school is from Section 8. That's an even fancier term for Government Assistance Housing. The way I figure it, in my neighborhood, you're either at a low-income school, or you're at a fancy-pants private school.

At private school in Portland, every day is fancy. They have *variety* in their cafeteria. Do you want pasta or pizza? A hamburger or a sandwich? Hot chocolate with whipped cream or marshmallows?

That's nothing like Washington. We get whatever they plop onto our plates, and we don't get any choices. The teachers are trying, but the security guards are all watching us like hawks. Checking bags and dumping books. So uncool. They don't want you going home with more than you came in with. Just a good education, not all the paperclips. It's a good idea, but it doesn't work. Someone stole our pencil sharpener last week. Now, we have to walk to Mr. Arndt's room to sharpen pencils.

Dad wrote some grant to get us on this trip. It was a big deal. T-shirts and everything. He even got us bottles of water with bright blue labels.

Jaiden knocked my shoulder. "Cool t-shirt, bro."

"Yours is awesome."

"Thanks," I said, puffing out my chest.

It really wasn't, but Jaiden and I had on the same bright yellow field trip shirts. We were the same height and the same weight, but Jaiden had that long dark hair, and you could see his mom in his features. His skin is a lot darker than mine. I guess I'm somewhere in-between my mom and dad.

Jaiden snapped me with his rubber band. "Dare you to ride the T-Rex," he said.

I grabbed for his rubber band, but he ripped it away. "What do I win?" I asked instead.

"My undying love."

"How about tacos?"

"How many?"

Jaiden smiled. "Five."

"Deal."

"Deal?" Jules asked. "Really Gwyn? You'd actually ride the T-Rex? You'd get yourself in that much trouble for five tacos?"

"He's not Gwyn," Jaiden said, holding the door open for us with a bow. "He's Wylde! Wa-hoooo! This field trip is gonna rule!"

Jaiden ran down the hall.

"Slow down!" Mr. Riker said. Jaiden saluted him as he sailed by. "*Por supuesto.*"

Riker rolled his eyes and turned to glare at me and Jules. I think he's hired to look mad at us. Before he could start anything again, we were out the door and in the parking lot.

Jaiden spun and jumped onto the bus, nearly colliding with Mrs. Klein. She just smiled, shaking her head and checking him off on her clipboard. She nodded at Jules, the corners of her eyes crinkling, but her brow furrowed the moment she caught my eye.

"You doing okay?" she asked.

"Yep!"

"He pack you a lunch?"

"Nope!"

She sighed as I slipped past her. I wasn't worried. He'd get me something at OMSI, or Jules would share with me.

I scanned the bus. Jules was already sitting by Jaiden, so I looked for a seat next to them. No luck. There was one open next to Kai, and one right next to my dad. I kept my head down so Dad wouldn't see me, pulled off my backpack, and slid in next to Kai.

Kai already had his book open. He didn't look up.

"What are you reading?" I asked.

He stared down at the page. "Your dad's wrong."

That's how Kai talked. We're all used to it. As he's told us before, he's autistic, so he communicates in a way that's comfortable with him. He's pretty straightforward.

But, here's the kicker: his dad is my dad's boss at Dad's second job, which makes things a thousand times more awkward.

"Yep," I said. "Dad is wrong all the time. But what about, specifically?"

"He's obsessed with the first law of thermodynamics. But that's all about isolated systems. And we don't *live* in an isolated system. We live in a galaxy, a universe, of possibilities. I could punch you, and the energy from that impact could disturb the air – the neurons in the oxygen particles themselves – through your body and all the way into outer space."

"Why would you punch me?"

Kai looked up then, a faint smile on his lips. "They say humor is the premier coping mechanism. Humans love to laugh in the face of frustration and loss."

I squeezed my hands together in my lap, brown skin stretching to white under the pressure. "What's that mean?"

"It means you've had practice with grief. Death. You've learned to cope."

Suddenly, punching those neurons into outer space sounded like an excellent idea. "You suck, Kai."

"Anger is another way to cope."

"That explains why I want to hit you."

He slammed his notebook shut and spun toward me. "You can feel it, right? That burn of energy in your chest? That's your cardiovascular response kicking in. Did you know that angry people are three times more likely to have a heart attack? It's all those catecholamines encouraging fatty deposits in your heart."

I took a deep breath, and felt the pounding of my heart deep in my chest. He was right. Something was happening in there. "Why do you know that?"

"My dad had a heart attack."

My tongue stuck in my mouth. "Is that why you were gone?"

"Yes."

"I'm sorry."

"I'm not."

"Wow. What?"

"He needs to make a substantial lifestyle change. He is often angry, but he lacks control of his anger. You work through your anger in therapy, yes?"

I snorted. "That's an understatement."

"I find it a useful tool."

"Okay," I said. I tapped my leg twice, then looked away.

He bowed his head down to his book again.

Done talking. For now. He'd probably start again soon. I pulled out my journal and started a list.

2

OMSI IS RIGHT DOWN ON THE WATERFRONT, WITH A REAL US Navy submarine docked next to it, right there in the Willamette River. Dad doesn't like to tour it because he says it costs like 800 dollars, but that's okay because there's always something to do there, even on the weekends. One of these days I'll convince him to let me bring Jaiden, and we'll have more fun and read less exhibit signs.

It's not so bad, though. The whole place is built for kids. Honestly. OMSI is like someone designed two average brick office buildings and then they let a toddler come through and decorate with glass and tiles and bright red smokestacks.

Dad loves it. His face lights up every time we walk through the door. Which is different than when we're at home and that blankness wraps around him. I swear, at night, his glasses are the only part of him that's real.

That day, his face glowed in the reflection of the sun through the glass. Standing in front of us, he raised his hands toward the ceiling. "This, my friends, is a place of possibility. So much to explore. Look at the T-Rex, the submarine in the river, and the Turbine Hall. Take it all in. There is so much to understand! So much to learn! I want to take you right to thermo-dynamics—"

The class groaned, and Mrs. Klein cleared her throat.

"But Mrs. Klein informs me that we have tickets for the Dr. Who exhibit at ten—"

"Yes!"

I didn't even have to look. I knew that was Jules.

Dad sighed. "There is time for everything." He shook his head. "Though Einstein tells us that time is an illusion." Mrs. Klein waved her hand at him. "So, to the exhibit we go."

Jules bounced up next to me, and we made our way through the entrance and down the hallway, walking along the lines in the tiles.

"I don't really get it," I said. "Why is there a Dr. Who exhibit here anyway? Isn't this a science museum?"

Dad turned back toward us. "I won't ruin it for you, Gwyn." I focused my eyes ahead, and walked a little slower up the stairs, hoping he'd take the hint. He didn't. His eyes gleamed brighter instead. "But science fiction is always on the forefront of exploration and innovation. Take a moment and consider..."

I swallowed, preparing for his lecture. I didn't have to listen to him at home, but I did at school. He was real strict about it. He pink-slipped me at the beginning of the year – sent me straight to the principal. He got me five more times before I finally gave in.

I couldn't get away from him. It's so annoying having your dad as a teacher. I mean, he has that second job at Flicker. If he only worked there he wouldn't have to follow me around at school too. But we need the money because of the stupid medical bills.

I watched the Willamette River flowing outside the windows. At least we were on a field trip.

He was on a roll, his teacher brain expanding by the second. "The transmitters they used in Star Trek—"

"Communicators," Jules interrupted.

"Yes. The communicators. They seemed beyond possibility during the first Star Trek—"

"The Original Series," Jules added.

"Yes, yes," Dad said. "But now we have mobile phones, which are the same technology—"

"Actually," Jules interrupted, "the closer comparison would be satellite phones, since the communicators aren't using cell phone towers."

Dad stopped in front of us. "Excuse me, Jules. Did you want to finish this explanation for me?"

Dad looked over the edge of his glasses at her, and she tugged on the arm of her hoodie, pulling it down further over her prosthesis, but then she nodded her head slightly. "Kind of?"

Jaiden laughed behind us, and Dad threw him a look, then sighed, turned, and continued toward the exhibit. "Be my guest," he said over his shoulder.

"Thank you," Jules said. "Okay. So, remember the ninth episode of the new Dr. Who?"

"Who?" Jaiden asked, and I laughed.

"What?" I asked, and Jaiden snorted.

"Come on," Jules said. "That joke is so old. I'm talking about the ninth episode. We just watched it over Christmas."

I scratched my head. "Is that the one where Dr. Who keeps not understanding stuff? Or falling in love? Or almost getting people killed? Or really getting them killed?"

"Exterminate!" Jaiden said, and Jules laughed.

"You both get so wrapped up in the Daleks. I'm talking about the one with the nano genes, remember? From the alien warship? They can heal people from the inside. And the thing is, that technology – it's not so far off anymore. Scientists have been working on nanobots – tiny robots that swim through your veins—"

"Gross!" Jaiden said.

"And bring therapy," Jules continued. "Medicine. Healing. Imagine the possibilities. People wouldn't get so sick. They wouldn't have to have chemo. They wouldn't—"

She stopped then.

Of course she stopped then. Her words melted as we walked up to the entrance to the exhibit.

"Sorry," she whispered.

"It's fine," I said.

"It's not," she said.

"I think it's gross," Jaiden said as we passed the ticket taker.

"Jaiden!" Jules said, and smacked him in the arm. He tried to hit her with his rubber band.

"Me too," I added. "Super gross."

"It's science, Wylde." Her eyes narrowed, then locked on the glittering screwdriver handles fixed onto the exhibit door. "Now, be quiet."

When Mom died, Dad built a wall out of his grief. Brick by brick, he took all of the happiness and all of the stories and everything that was good about Mom and us and he balled it all up and crumpled it and turned it into lab notes and research and dumb dumb dumb dumb.

My therapist told Dad to spend time with me. Real time together, without movies or TV or pizza. Talking time. She actually wrote it out on her prescription pad. Told Dad she wasn't

He couldn't stand to be in
the house alone with me. He
needed to **DO**. Needed to **GO**.
Plus, he got a stupid second
job. He had to. After Mom died,
after the visitation and the
funeral and the burial and the
standin around and and once
everybody finally left and all the
casseroles
and the pies
were gone,
that's when
I saw them. The medical bills stacked
on the kitchen table. He ignored them
for a while until they started calling
and he couldn't ignore them anymore.
He got a second job at Flicker, working
weeknights and Saturdays, which left
Sunday at OMSI.

It's the only place I've seen him
smile since Mom left.

3

"Before we get started, remember to answer the questions we wrote down in your lab notebook if you want credit for today's assignment."

Jules was bouncing on the balls of her feet and swinging her arms in the air. Her red hair flew in her face, and she pushed it back again. Jaiden was snapping his rubber band into my leg. Nobody cared about lab notebooks. I don't think I even brought a pen. Mrs. Klein waved Dad on.

"Let's go," she said. My palms were getting sweaty. Dad's foot tapped the tile. Mrs. Klein smiled. "We don't want to miss our tour. Okay, crew. Have fun, pay attention, and most of all—"

"Be kind," we said, and she finally opened the doors.

A long, narrow hallway led into the darkness.

Jules rushed in, with Jaiden right behind her.

I hesitated at the door, my breath catching. I tried to smooth it out, but it caught again. The walls ahead were narrow, tight. Were they leaning in? No. Just a normal hallway. It was fine. Was it fine? I tried to take a breath. Nope. Not fine.

I cut out of line and walked over to Dad. My head was spinning. I couldn't catch my breath.

"Bathroom," I choked out. Why? Why was this happening now?

His fake smile disappeared. "Now?"

"Now."

I sucked in a breath. It came in hot. He still hadn't looked at me. He was watching the other kids file through the doors. I wheezed in another bite of air.

"I wish you wouldn't do this," he said quietly.

"What?" I asked. I couldn't focus. Couldn't think. How could he, when I, why would he? Why?

I cleared my throat, anxiety turning to anger. Heat rolled up my face. My breath came in easier. Cleaner.

I glared up at him, but he didn't see – wouldn't look at me. "Hey," I said. He wasn't looking. "Mr. Wylde." Still not looking. I waved my hand in front of him. "I'm over here." He finally looked down at me. My mind cleared as I looked into his narrowed brown eyes. "And I have to go to the bathroom."

"Alright," he said, pulling that fake smile back on.

My hand dropped to my side and tightened into a fist. In that moment, he wasn't a teacher. He was a dad. And he had no idea how to do that.

"You know where to go," he said. "Meet us inside."

I spun away from him, my fingernail pressed into my palm, all my weird anxiety replaced by anger. Geez. It's awkward enough being in his class. Why can't he just believe me when I say I have to pee? I'm in middle school, not Kindergarten.

It should be a rule. You shouldn't have your dad as a teacher. Middle school is hard enough. You need time to yourself. More air. More space to breathe. To think.

I needed to talk to Geneva. I'd tell her about school and about Dad – how nothing was working – how he was sad all the time. No, not sad...empty. He was not there anymore.

She'd help me. Even if we couldn't fix the big stuff, we could at least find some way to get me out of Dad's class. She would listen. She'd understand. And she'd try to help.

Switching to B schedule wouldn't be so bad. I could take Gershow's class. I'd do it if they let me stay in my other classes with Jaiden and Jules. Sure, Mrs. Gershow is a super hard grader, and the rest of the year would be absolute torture, but at least she isn't my dad.

I headed toward the bathroom. It wasn't very far – just across the hall. Okay, fine. I didn't have to pee – I just needed some space. I couldn't breathe in that exhibit. Everything was so tight. And hot.

It was all so wrong. I wasn't even supposed to be in Dad's class, on his stupid field trip. I just turned 12 last week. Things were supposed to be different – better. I slammed my hand against the door. They weren't. They weren't better.

And they were never going to be.

Geneva gave me this journal last year, and we made a deal. I only had to see her once a month, as long as I wrote in my journal every day. She said that research has shown a greater increase in perceived happiness with people who journal every day. I told her perceived happiness doesn't sound super reassuring. She said that's just how I perceive it.

DUMB At first, I thought it was **dumb**. She said I should write that. So I did. I wrote it was dumb every day for ten days. That was a lot of dumb.

DUMB
D U M B

DUMB

DUMB

DUMB

DUMB

DUMB

DUMB

DUMB

DUMB

Tiny dumb

DUMB

DUMB

Then I wrote about pancakes with syrup. Basketball. Chocolate. Music. Superheroes. After a while, I got used to writing every day. And, well, I kind of started to like it. I know it sounds super weird, but all those words actually have helped things make sense.

Except, you know, Mom's death. That still doesn't make any sense. None at all. I don't think it ever will.

And then there's all those months she spent in the hospital bed or in the bathroom.

All of that still sucks. A lot. But I'm writing it down, and I'm not as mad. I think. Sometimes.

Anyways, this counts for today. So that's cool.

Still a little dumb.

4

Here's the deal. Monday was my birthday. Yes, the big one – I turned twelve years old. I'd been waiting for that day for years – since I was a little kid. I know it sounds dumb, but I thought it was going to happen.

It was the last piece of her I had left. The last story. The one that mattered.

It had dug down so far into me that I couldn't help but expect it. She promised – told me night after night. The spark. From the other side of the mountain. It would happen.

But it didn't. Nothing happened. At all. I woke up. I got dressed. Nana came over. She made waffles. I walked to school. Jaiden gave me a pack of Magic cards. Jules bought me tacos. We played basketball after school. It was a good day. An easy day.

It should have been a happy day. But it wasn't, because nothing *happened*. No dramatic floating into the air. No bursting into the sky. No rising. No flying.

No wings.

It's stupid. I know it's stupid. People can't fly. That's not a thing. It was just a dumb story that Mom had made up a long time ago to get me to fall asleep and I shouldn't have listened to her. I shouldn't have thought it was real.

I should have just swallowed it down and went to bed like she was telling me the story of *The Three Little Pigs* or *Little Red Riding Hood.*

But Mom never told me those stories. Until the day I walked into elementary school, I had never heard a single nursery rhyme. I thought Mother Goose was a just store in downtown Portland.

You see, Mom never told me about little pigs – she wove the tale of the wild boar that killed Diarmuid. She didn't scare me with stories of Nana-eating wolves – she told me about her Nana who *was* a wolf – who ate little kids for breakfast. Her stories were so beautiful and magic and wild and raw that they didn't seem at all possible.

But there was something about that story with the wings. Something that rang true, deep inside me. Something that seemed right.

So I hoped...just maybe...

I threw open the bathroom door and stumbled into the room, my breath disappearing from my chest. I grabbed the edges of the sink and tried to open back up, but my eyes tightened, my chest flared—

No. I wouldn't cry. Not in the stupid bathroom of OMSI. Not on a field trip. And definitely not about this.

I sucked in a breath and tried to push it back out, but it stuck, and the tears began to fall, wet against my face.

I sucked in a ragged breath, and pushed it back out, again and again, trying to find my way to the other side.

Once again, those breaths are the reason why stories suck. Mom had me believing — she had me honestly thinking — after all this time—

I pushed my face into my sleeve, wiped my arm across my eyes. I needed to get back. Back to the field trip. Back to Dr.

Who, back to time travel, and back to the Science of Possibility. Back to Dad and his dumb research. Back to Jules who is probably freaking out with joy. Back to Jaiden who has no one to hit with his rubber band. Back to life with my feet on the ground, without the memory – the possibility – of something else.

I looked up at my face in the mirror, my puffy red eyes, the streaks on my brown cheeks, and just then, I caught a glint of light on the toilet stall behind me. I blinked, and it flickered. It sparked, and grew bigger. Right over my shoulder.

I spun around, but nothing was there. No spark, no reflection. Just a shining silver bathroom and a stupid crying kid. A weird sound jumped out of my mouth as I stared at my wavy reflection. Not a whimper, or a cry. Not a laugh.

It was the sound of emptiness.

Just like Dad.

Nothing left. I was turning into him. And all those pieces of Mom were gone.

I wiped my face again on my sleeve and turned back toward the faucet.

Light pushed into my eyes. It was brilliant – a shining, pulsing golden star, spinning and twirling through the air. How – what? My eyes narrowed and it flashed forward faster. It sparked off my reflection and headed straight toward me.

I fell backwards into the toilet stall.

It couldn't be—

It wasn't—

It was.

It burst out of the mirror. I dove to the side, and it slammed into the stall, crushing the metal straight into the toilet. Water exploded into the air, spraying the side of my face and hair, and knocking my glasses off my face.

Feet slipping, scrambling, I grabbed the door handle and threw it open. When I glanced back, the ball of light was flying right toward me.

"What?" I yelled, breaking across the hallway and running toward the screwdriver doors. The light pulled in front of me and forced me up the stairs instead.

"Help!" I yelled at the ticket taker.

He just scowled at me. "No running in the museum."

"No running in the museum?" I yelled down the stairs. "There's a giant ball of death chasing me! And you don't want me to run in the museum?"

He just shook his head as I rounded the turn.

Why wasn't he calling for help? Why wasn't he chasing after me? That thing was gonna kill me.

I ran past the Science Playground on the second floor. I didn't want to be trapped in there. I could hit the stairs on the other side, and make my way back down. With the light nipping at my heels, I turned the corner and cut down the back stairs, sprinting by the Science Store. I burst into the Main Lobby. The T-Rex shot into the sky, its bones reflecting the sunlight.

Perfect. The place was packed with kids. I could easily lose the light in the crowd and make my way back to the exhibit hall and to Dad. He'd know what to do. I just had to move fast. I spun past a small group and curved around the rope line, weaving in and out of the crowd. I turned back to see the light hovering by the stairs. I slowed down. I stiffened up. I stopped.

It was impossible. I was going crazy. Insane. There wasn't a ball of light chasing me. It wasn't even real.

I blinked my eyes and rubbed them hard. I looked away from the light, then glanced back. Still there, golden and flickering. It didn't disappear. In fact, it spun in a circle, then narrowed into an eye which flipped around, and then looked directly at me.

I fell back against the ropes, panting hard. How was this happening? I had to get away. New plan. Take the other exit.

I checked my path to break into a run, then glanced back at

the light. And – as if it all wasn't weird enough – here's the weirdest part: I swear, it winked at me.

I turned and ran right into a tall man with dark hair.

"Excuse me—"

"That ball of light—" I began.

He steadied himself and tilted his head. His son pulled on his other arm. "I don't—"

"See! It's right there!"

It flew toward me, weaving and spinning through the crowd, up and over the info desk.

"It's there!" I yelled. "Look up! It's right there on top of the registration sign!"

The man shook his head. "Where are sus padres? You can't just—" His son broke away and bolted toward the door. "Frankie!" he yelled. "Espere!" He ran after him.

I watched him push through the crowd. "Dad," I said. "I have to get back to Dad." I sprinted to the side and skidded past a group of kids. "Move!" I yelled. They looked at me like I was crazy. I probably was. But I had to get away.

A hand grabbed my arm. "You need to come with me."

Tall. Grey-haired. In a suit. Security? He looked familiar. But he wasn't wearing an OMSI shirt. Wait.

"Mr. Wythe?" I asked.

Dad's boss. What was he doing here? Was he on the bus? He was Kai's dad too. Maybe he was chaperoning.

"Gwyn," he snapped.

"Yes!" I yelled. "Yes! Me. Help! There's a ball of—"

"Please stop making a scene," Wythe said.

"Argh! Don't you see it?" I asked, pointing at the ball whizzing toward us.

"I don't see anything but an out of control kid—"

I ripped my arm free, dove to the side, and nearly collided with a real security guard.

The ball of light was sweeping the edge of the room toward

me, so I didn't even try with the real security guard. He put out his arm, and I pushed past it, ran around him, and went back for the center. I'd wrap around the T-Rex and hit the door on the other side. All I needed to do—

Nope. The light was right behind me with the man in the suit. "Seriously?" It was fast. I jumped the rail around the T-Rex and the alarm blared. I ran underneath the T-Rex's leg bones, but the guard was coming right for me too, so I grabbed a hold of the rib bone, wrenched my legs up, and pulled myself right into the T-Rex's rib cage. The golden light flashed by me, then whipped back around.

It was getting worse and worse. The alarm screeched, the grey-haired suit was grabbing for my legs, and the light was zooming right toward me. I jerked to the side, then climbed up through the ribcage toward the tippy-top of the dinosaur.

I know what you're thinking. You're thinking, why are you climbing *up* the T-Rex? Well, I'm not very good at stressful situations, okay? I was trying to get away from that insane ball of light, and the guards wouldn't leave me alone, and by that point, I was standing on the shoulders of the T-Rex, and the light was zooming up its tail, coming right for me, and I couldn't think with the scream of the alarm, so I scrambled up the T-Rex's head, intending to climb down its jaw and drop to the floor, but when I got there, I did the thing you're never supposed to do—

I looked down.

I'm not scared of heights. But I am scared of falling from them. And I didn't have my glasses on and everything looked just a little fuzzy and all those windows were shining sunlight down on the faces of the crowd and sparkling off of my impending doom. So, way deep in the pit of my stomach, something churned and twisted, and my head went all woozy, and my eyes started to blur. Then my knees got all squishy, and—

"Gwyn!"

I turned to meet Dad's eyes across the room.

"What are you—" He stopped, and his hand shot out, pointing right at the ball of light.

He could see it. He could see it! I wasn't going crazy. There really was a giant ball of light — headed right for my chest.

It slammed into me, sizzling right through my shirt. For a moment, my chest filled with warmth and light. Then my feet left the ground, the bones exploded beneath me, and I flew up and into the air — streaking backward — fire running through my chest, over my shoulders, and down my back, until I crashed into the highest window.

The glass shattered around me, scraping my face and arms, but not slowing me down. I twisted and hurtled toward the ground, spinning, spinning, spinning, and screaming. I wrapped my arms around my head, but right before I crashed into the ground, I threw my hands out in front of me and my shoulders wrenched up and my back wrenched too and something inside me broke free and lifted up and pulled me into the sky.

My mind spun as I glided over the dock, past the submarine, and down toward the Willamette River. The wind wrapped around me, cutting through my hair and my clothes.

I soared through the sky, face first into the wind.

I was flying.

"When?" I asked.
"12," she said. "When you're 12."

I paused, thinking. "You were 12."
"I was."

My face turned up to her. "Where are your wings?"

"I used them all up," she said softly. "I needed all of my magic to make you. But don't worry. I will get them back someday."

"How?"

"Kindness magic. Simple things. Smiling. Hugging. Being good to each other. All of that wonderful stuff you do every day...it helps your wings grow."

"What's it like?" I asked. "To fly?"

She smiled. "It's like the sky wraps you in a warm, fuzzy blanket, fresh out of the dryer, and pulls you up, folding you in. It's like freedom and pudding and all the things you love. It's a million perfect things, all at once. It's like you're finally free.

FREE*

*For a limited time only.

5

SOMETHING WAS CARRYING ME THROUGH THE AIR. I COULD FEEL IT pulling against my back, stretching out my skin. I turned my head to see what had a hold of my hoodie, what had rescued me from becoming squashed pavement, but all I saw was great, big, dazzling white feathers and stretched out wings. A bird. There was a bird stuck on me! I turned all the way around to get a better look, but suddenly, I was free-falling, the bird's wings wrapping around me and my chest.

"Get off me!" I yelled. "Bird!" Feathers and straining. Stretching and pulling, tighter and tighter, covering my face, my mouth, and then—

Water.

Why you should never swim in the

Willamette River

* It's cold
* It's wet.
* It's super-polluted.
* You never know what you're going
to find underwater. There could be
leeches, or piranhas, or man-eating
whales. Or there could be sharks.

With jaws and teeth, so many teeth.
I mean, have you seen Shark Week?
Those things are vicious. You wouldn't
last a second against a shark. It
wouldn't just eat your body...it would
consume your soul. Did you hear about
that guy surfing in Hawaii? He's not
surfing anymore. Because he's dead.
Because a shark ate him.
* Did I mention it's cold?

6

I FOUGHT AGAINST THE DIRTY WATER, SHOVING AT THE FEATHERS and digging for the surface. Pump. Push. Air. Needed air. My lungs burned hot. I opened my eyes. Darkness below. And above. Everywhere. Which way was up? Down? All muddy. Feathers. Air. Blue light! Forward. Move! Up. Up!

I broke the surface and coughed out water, then gulped down air. Air! Water flooded in, and I coughed it out, spitting into the river, sniffing and breathing and swimming, barely swimming. I'm good at swimming, but not with all my clothes and a weird giant bird weighing me down. So, I freaked out. Wagging my arms, moving my legs, trying to find the shore. My hoodie was all bunched up, and my legs were so heavy. I saw a tree and started kicking my feet hard toward it, but the stupid bird was still on my back, its feathers dripping, gripping onto my shoulders and arms. I hit its wings away, but it pushed back harder, and I was tired. So tired.

I focused on swimming toward the shore. My clothes, my body, so tired, so heavy, so wet. Push, kick, splash, move. Just keep moving. Don't stop. Go forward. Kick.

When I finally got close enough, I put my feet down on the muddy bank and trudged through the rest of the water, dragging my legs toward the beach, toward the sand, then I fell down to my hands and knees, gasping, chest heaving, pulling in air.

"Breathe," I said, like it would make the air come faster. "Just breathe," I repeated, shivering as my wet shirt dripped down my chest through the hole in the front. "You're fine. You're okay."

I stared down at the sand. Blood dripped down from a huge gash on my arm. When did I get it? The window. I crashed through a window. My face hurt too – I needed a Band-Aid. Or a nap.

I rolled over onto my back. The bird kicked and flapped its wings against me.

"Stupid bird!" I yelled, rolling off it. I tried to lay on my side, but it squirmed beneath me, jerking against my arms. "Come on!" I had to get it off. I pulled myself to my feet, and blood rushed to my head as the world spun around me. I closed my eyes, then forced them open again. Not yet. After the bird. I'd be able to lay down once I got it off my back. I lifted my arms up to pull it off, and its wing stuck tight to my shoulder. I jerked my arm away, but weirdly, it did too.

"What?"

I pulled up my other arm, and its other wing was stuck to that arm like a bad Big Bird suit.

"Come on! Seriously?"

I flapped both my arms, trying to get it off me, and — I swear — my feet left the ground. My breath caught, then stuck deep in my throat. I coughed hard into my elbow, and fell back to the sand again.

"Bird," I said. "Stupid bird."

Something, an idea, stirred in the back of my mind, deep-down, and started pushing its way forward in my brain. But I refused to listen to it. I couldn't. It was a bird. Just a stupid bird. It couldn't be—

I squinted and caught a reflection from a truck in the nearby parking lot.

I ran for it, arms pumping, feet stumbling, and those wet feathers sloshing behind me.

I stopped in front of the truck trailer. I raised my hands. The feathers dripped down behind me, and that line of blood made its way down my arm. I closed my eyes.

Slowly, I turned my head, arms spread. I couldn't feel the cold anymore. For a long moment, my eyes stayed closed. I didn't want to see. Didn't want to know. It wasn't possible. It couldn't be. Then my eyes shot open, and I looked at my reflection behind me.

It wasn't a stupid bird.

I had my wings.

Drawing of Me
(with wings!)

7

I RAISED MY ARMS HIGH, SPREADING MY WINGS UP INTO THE AIR. It didn't seem possible. It wasn't possible. It couldn't be. It was just a story. It wasn't real.

I probably busted my head. I fell against that window and broke something important.

Or maybe the whole light thing never even happened. Maybe I really passed out on the bathroom floor.

Maybe I was dead.

I ripped off my soaking wet hoodie, dropping it on the ground, and looked at my bloody arm, my soggy hair, the hole in my shirt.

Maybe I splattered the pavement.

That idea caught me for a moment. It was the only one that made any sense. I had died. I had turned into an angel with incredible white wings—

And blood dripping down my arm. I grabbed the front of my t-shirt and ripped the hole downward, pulling and then tearing off the bottom of my shirt. I took the long strap and slowly wound it around my arm, then tied it in a knot. Dead or whatever, it seemed wrong to just let my arm keep bleeding.

Wait, you don't bleed when you're dead. You get, like rigor mortis or something, right? A dream, then. Probably a dream. Yeah, that would make sense. After all those stories, after all the waiting, and after my 12th birthday, so much stress, that was the most obvious possibility, of course. I was dreaming.

I folded the wings around me and then back out again.

"So cool," I whispered.

I shook them, and sparkling drops of water cascaded down to the ground. Real wings. My wings.

Dream or not, they were pretty cool.

A low horn broke across the water, then sirens blared, long and loud. Headed to OMSI, no doubt. I looked out across the water and smiled. Who cared about OMSI? That submarine could sink. This was a billion times better. I was having the best dream in the history of ever.

I shook out my wings like a dog at the beach. I probably only had a couple more minutes before I woke up, and why waste them standing around in the sand?

I needed to fly. But how?

A duck, flapping its wings – I could do that. I lifted my arms up and down, and the wings followed along with them. They weren't actually attached to my arms, but they trailed along after them.

It was harder than I thought. The wings were heavy – they stretched and pulled against my shoulders, drawing out muscles I never knew I had. My clothes were wet and cold, and each bend of my wing kicked up gravel around my shoes and air swished against my naked stomach, but then, with a swirl of rocks and dirt, my feet were no longer on the ground. One inch, then a foot, then a yard: each flap of my wings brought me up higher, until I passed over the tops of the trees and looked out over the river to the opposite bank. A huge black dog ran along the dock, and a flash of lights almost blinded me – red, blue, and pulsing. So many police. Firefighters. And strangely, a black car speeding away from the museum like a bolt of lightning flashing over the ground.

If I went toward the OMSI, the dream would turn bad super-fast – dogs and policemen and a really angry dad. Besides all that, I'd wake up, sweating and panting in my bed. Then I'd have to do the field trip all over again – without the wings.

So I flapped my wings toward the interstate, caught the sign for 26, and followed it over to the zoo.

The zoo would be packed in two weeks, but it was May 1st, and still chilly at the end of the work week. Once I got there, it would be smooth sailing.

I swallowed and flapped harder as I passed the few skyscrapers on the northwest edge of Portland. I was so exposed – nothing but me, the clouds, and the sky.

If someone looked out their office window, they'd see a kid with wings and a torn shirt, flapping his arms madly, trying to stay in the air and simultaneously out of sight.

I flapped my wings harder, the cold wind cut into my face, and I banked left and lower toward the interstate. I tried to fly high enough that the cars didn't see me, but low enough that I didn't lose my way. I was tempted to hop on a skyscraper and act like King Kong, but instead I flew over the tunnel, caught the exit, and zoomed by the zoo.

Finally. There it was – Forest Park – one of the largest urban forests in the United States. It ran for miles along the west side of the city. It was exactly what I needed.

My body thrummed as I broke out over the forest, caught the wind, and glided through the air. I banked left and then right, twirled to the side, then shouted as I flipped over. I dove down toward the trees, then pulled up quickly and straightened out, flying straight for the horizon.

Blue above and green below.

Free.

Finally free.

It was just like Mom said – wrapped in a blanket of stars and launched into the sky. No Dad, no homework, no laws or equations. Just me, hands open, fingers stretched out, banking toward the horizon. Toward life, toward possibility, toward freedom. I took a deep breath, and it filled me to the top.

No one could catch me, no one could stop me. The sky was made of dreams.

Mom once told me that heaven is a story that's been told a thousand times, but we don't really know what it's going to be like until we get there. Sure, there's paintings of shiny angels and fluffy, white clouds in an endless, eternally infinite blue sky, but that's just our **idea** of heaven.

Heaven?

"In Welsh Mythology, there's no real heaven," Mom told me. "There's no eternal home you have to **earn**. Everyone goes to the Otherworld. It's ruled by Arawn, and he's powerful. Angry. He lives with his demons and angels in a world of earthly delight."

"Angels and demons?" I asked. "Together?"

"Of course. Most celtic mythology doesn't have a heaven or hell. That came in later. In the beginning, there was just the Otherworld: the place you go when you die. No sin, no punishment. That's not the Celtic way."

I never really liked Mom's version
of heaven and hell...all those wide-
mawed beasts and demons dancing
beside elven maidens. I liked the
picture-perfect version of heaven.

White clouds, blue skies, and those giant, shining pearly gates. Nothing to be afraid of anymore. Nothing to keep us apart. No Arawn, no demons. No more death. Just all of us. Together.

Heaven.

8

COLD.

It snuck up on me, sneaking deep into my skin and down into my bones. So cold. A shiver ran down my back. There was a reason people weren't headed to the zoo. The spring wind was freezing — biting into my wet clothes and crashing into my stomach. Why did I rip off the bottom of my shirt? Stupid Incredible Hulk moment. I didn't think the dream would last so long.

I needed to wake myself up. I reached over to pinch my arm, but forgot my wings, and rolled through the sky until I caught myself and leveled out again.

Okay. No pinching. I closed my eyes tight and opened them again. Still flying.

I bit my lip. Hard. Harder. Didn't matter. Still soaring through the air.

I stared out at the trees covering the horizon. If this was real, I'd made a terrible mistake. But this couldn't be real. I was flying over Forest Park. In the air. With wings. Was this really real?

I needed a nap. I needed a Pepsi. I needed some tacos.

Focus, Wylde.

Feet first. Nap second. Tacos third.

I looked down at the trees beneath me, eyes tracking across the field of endless forest that flowed past the edge of my sight. I wished I still had my glasses on. Everything was just this side of smudgy.

I couldn't land in a tree. My wings would get stuck and I'd tumble to the ground and break all my feathers. And my head. I'd have to find an open field or a parking lot.

If I made my way to the river, I'd probably end up in St. John's? Dad had taken me to a cool bookstore there. They also had a lot of yarn. It was all very Portland.

If the yarn pile was big enough, I could land on that, but the dream wasn't giving me large piles of yarn. It was giving me wings. And I was getting tired. But if I hit St. John's, maybe I could plop down by one of those warehouses. Their roofs would be like a landing strip. Now, where was the river? Left? Right?

East.

Which way was east again?

I had no clue. I'd been twirling and spinning and cutting through the air, banking left and right. I hadn't gone straight ahead – I'd been testing my wings. Plus, I spun around when I pinched myself too. I think. I don't know. Which way? I looked back toward the horizon. That way?

And I was tired. So tired. I had to keep going – I was flying over a solid block of forest. Why did I choose the forest? What if I fell? I almost drowned before. Can you die in a dream? Get stuck in a tree? I was going to find out. Stupid way to die. Climbing trees the wrong way. I was running out of options though. The wings on my back were like giant weights that could also get stuck on stuff or suffocate me if I fell in the water. I was toast. And not the kind with jelly.

Peanut butter and jelly. On wheat. That would be good. It wouldn't take as long as tacos.

I shook my head. Focus. The sun. Rises in the east, sets in the west. I looked toward the sky. I was in the sky. It was grey. Where was the sun? Why was there no sun? Too many clouds. The sun had to be up there somewhere. I could fly higher? Up over the clouds? But it would be crazy cold up there. With, like, space and stuff. There probably wasn't any air there either.

I needed to go south. Back to OMSI.

No. I needed to get on the ground. It didn't matter which direction I went. Get on the ground. Down through the forest. The tree. Reverse tree climbing, from the top down. Here we go!

I cut down toward the canopy.

Woozy. Tired. Arms so heavy.

A flash of gold. A smack against my right wing. I twisted my head, flapping my heavy arms.

Owl.

"Hoot."

Owl? Why was there an owl?

"Hoot!"

Okay. It was hooting at me. That made sense. It would probably start talking soon. Tell me about my quest. Or disappear. Really, I had wings. Anything could happen.

"Hoot."

I glanced at its wings. Its eyes flashed gold.

"Hoot."

"Alright, alright. You're an owl. And I'm losing my mind." It cut in front of me. I tried to push it away, but it batted off my hand and hooted. It was probably headed for some prey, and I was in the way. Or a weird owl party. It had plans.

I tried to fly around it, but it got all up in my face again, hooting and screeching, nudging me, pushing me.

Honestly, it seemed like it wanted me to go to the right – to follow it to the weird owl party.

It banked right, sharp and fast, and so did I, cutting directly into the wind.

"You sure?" I yelled. "It's colder this way. It's harder to fly into the wind, too!" It flew on, and I followed, green forest stretching out in front of us. The owl was focused on getting to that owl party – it shot through the sky, barely flapping its wings, while I struggled to keep mine going.

The owl was aerodynamic – sleek golden feathers pulled back, body pointed into the wind. It looked like it should be flying – like it was made for flying. Which it was.

And I wasn't. I was like a giant scarecrow that someone dressed in wet jeans and a torn shirt, filled with cement, then threw into the air, and yelled, "Flap your arms!"

Underwear. That's why superheroes wear tights and underwear. No extra flapping.

I laughed, feeling the strain of my shoulder muscles or back or whatever. My body was not made for this, and I definitely wasn't dressed right. But I'd never be caught dead with my underwear outside my clothes. How would I ever explain that one? And how did that help at all? Couldn't I just wear tights? I'd never wear tights though. They just put everything all out there. But maybe skinny jeans weren't such a terrible idea. They had to be more aerodynamic.

I caught a break in the horizon, a crack in the line of green. We flew toward it. The owl's path never wavered as the crack widened to reveal a river, with warehouses all along the waterfront.

"Yes!" I screamed, and headed right toward a parking lot next to a wide open field. I could force a landing, make it to the parking lot, and if I messed it up, I could roll into that field. And sleep for like 24 hours.

I aimed for the empty stretch of concrete, but the owl cut me off.

I pushed it out of the way. "Stop that!" I shouted.

It screeched and bit my arm.

"Ow! What are you doing?"

It pushed me again, nudging me, insisting.

I tricked it, spun to the right, but it cut off to the left, its claws cutting toward my eyes.

"Okay!" I shouted. "Okay!" Stupid owl. Stupid night. Stupid wings. Stupid guacamole.

Well, the wings were pretty cool. I was just wiped out from all the flying.

The owl came at me again.

"What?" I snapped. "Seriously!"

It turned its body toward the river, then flew back toward me, and turned its body to the river again. I followed its line of sight.

A rough shape broke the flow of the river, like a rock in the middle of a stream.

"What is that?"

Birds have good eyesight. Why couldn't I have good eyesight? I was kinda like a bird. Would I start tweeting? Or cheeping? Was I like a hawk? Would I scree through the sky? Or was I just going to hoot like an owl without a sucker?

Focus, Wylde. Focus.

I narrowed my eyes, and the shape on the river cleared up.

A boat.

I banked hard. Nope. People on boats. Not a good idea. Not gonna head toward—

The owl cut in front of me and then to my side, smacking its feathers in my face as it screeched by. "Stop it!" I spun out of the way and looked down. We were headed closer to the little speedboat. "I don't want to crash!"

I turned away again, and the owl was back in my face. I tried to push it away, but it just flipped around my head, and then we were even closer to the boat.

"What are you doing?" someone yelled. I narrowed my eyes, and saw the outline of a woman standing on the prow of the boat, yelling up at me. "Get down here right now!"

"Nana?" I yelled back.

Costume!

9

"YES," NANA YELLED. "IT'S ME. OF COURSE IT'S ME."

"Where'd you get that boat?"

"Are you going to land or not?"

Land. It sounded so good. My arms were shivering and trembling from the weight, and my back was on fire, stretched and scraped raw. Plus, I'm pretty sure I'd lost a lot of blood from crashing through that window.

"Yes! Okay. I'm coming!"

I flapped closer to the boat, but it was so tiny. There was barely any room for my feet, much less a landing.

"Come on, Gwyn."

"How?" I yelled down.

"Just get over here, and stop flapping those wings. You'll drop right in."

"Yeah, I'll miss the boat and drop right into the water!"

"I'll catch you!"

"No you won't."

"Darn right I won't. Now get down here."

I pulled up over the top of the boat and slowly lowered

myself down toward the back seat, then dropped my arms quickly. My stomach lurched, then I plopped into the boat.

Nana was staring down at me, her dark brown face scrunched up. Her hands sat on her hips. "Why were you flapping your arms like a chupacabra?"

I collapsed back into the seat, then rolled to the side, away from my wings. I was freezing cold. "Chupacabras don't have wings."

"I know that. What were you doing up there?"

"I was flying, Nana."

"Don't I know it. About time. But you don't need to flap your arms around like a baby in a haystack. You can move those wings on their own."

"How did you find me?"

"My owls."

"*Your* owls?"

The boat took off, and I grabbed the bar along the side. Nana was standing at the wheel, twisting it around. She was shorter than me, but nevertheless, she seemed to tower over me. I stared at her back, how she braced herself against the wind. Of course she was there. She was always right where I needed her. She was like a little Army sergeant, but always dressed in her Sunday best. You didn't mess with Nana. Nobody messed with Nana. If she told you to do something, you did it. Plain and simple.

The boat spun around, and I slid to the side, grabbing the bar with my other hand.

"Get that blanket in the chest behind you. You'll catch a chill. Where are your glasses?"

"OMSI," I mumbled, reaching behind me. I unclipped the silver clasp, and pulled out an old wool blanket. I wrapped it quickly around myself. It was scratchy, but it cut out the wind, and would block the water splashing against the bow. "Whose boat is this?"

"It's mine now."

"Where'd you get a boat?"

Nana swung her head back toward me. "Really?" she asked, her black braids whipping across her face. "That's what you're wondering about? You don't have, you know, any other questions?"

"Just one," I said, rubbing my face in the blanket. My wings trembled behind me. I looked up, and caught Nana's eye again. "Why do I have wings?"

Peach Dump Cake

* Turn oven to 375.
* Butter a big pan.
* Dump 1 big can of peaches into pan.
* Dump yellow cake mix on top.
* Push that down.
* Melt 1/2 cup butter.
* Pour the butter on top. No dry spots!
* Cook it for 50 minutes.
* Give it all to Gwyn.
* Repeat.

10

"YOU EVER LISTEN TO YOUR MOM'S STORIES?" NANA ASKED.

"Always," I said. It was freezing, so I pulled the blanket tight around my chest. Mom's stories made everything feel better. I remembered her whispered words and the covers tucked around me. I wished I was back there again. Warm and safe. "I listened. Every night."

"And you know there's a grain of truth in every story."

"Nana," I said with a sigh. "Come on. I have wings." I shook them gently, then tucked them back behind me again. "This isn't just a story. I. Have. Wings. People don't usually get wings."

"Some stories have more than a grain. Some stories have the entire casserole."

"That doesn't make any sense."

"It doesn't have to make sense. It just is. Besides, you're on YouTube."

"What?" I asked, dropping my blanket. "Where? Show me."

I crawled up and took the wheel from Nana. She pulled out her cell phone, and held onto the bar, squinting and tapping, then she handed it to me and took the wheel back. I leaned against the bar as the video started playing.

"Jaiden put it up."

I watched myself run up the top of the T-Rex. "Jaiden saw me fly?" I watched myself pause at the top of the T-Rex, staring into the crowd, then launching off into space.

"No. He saw you run up the T-Rex and shoot through a window."

I couldn't see the ball of light in the video, but I saw when it slammed into me and hurtled my body backward. The clip went by so fast. I crashed through the window and the video stopped. "What were you thinking, climbing around on that dinosaur?"

"I wasn't thinking! I was trying to get away from that murderous ball of light! Which, by the way, nobody saw! And is apparently inside me now?"

"You really need to learn to calm down. Be a tad more reasonable."

"Nana! There was a giant ball of light flashing toward me, it slammed me through a window, and then it gave me wings. Calm down? What are you even talking about?"

She turned and looked at me, and the lines on her face softened. "I'm sorry," she said. "This has to be overwhelming for you." She reached out, lightly touching a feather, and slowly smiled. "I really like your wings."

"Tell me a story."

"That's your mom's job," Dad said, tucking the covers in around me. "She's the storyteller."

"What's your job, then?"

"I'm a science teacher."

"Tell me science then."

I was only six years old. I thought science was a story, too.

"Okay," he said. "Let's talk about time." He pulled off his watch and handed it to me. I stared at the hands spinning round and round. "Watch the minute hand. You see it?"

"Which one?"

"The long one."

"Got it."

"You know we can count time. Quantify it. Track it. Observe it. Our observation tells us there are sixty seconds in one minute."

I only understood half the words he said, but I nodded my head anyway.

"But sixty minutes of video games goes by super quickly doesn't it?"

That I understood. I nodded my head bigger, swinging the watch back and forth and back again. "Way too fast."

"While sixty minutes in the car goes by so very slowly, doesn't it?"

"If you don't let me play with your phone," I said. "You should let me play with your phone more."

He nodded knowingly, reaching his hand back for the watch.

I grasped it tightly. "Why are you saying this science stuff?"

"Because we will always want more time. The important moments slip by us so quickly, especially these hours and minutes with your mom. Time is relative. Don't miss those moments. Pay attention."

I handed him back the watch. "Time is relative? Related to us?"

"Kind of. It's like you're playing tag with Jaiden. He keeps running away, or you do. That's time."

"Time is a game?"

He looked at me really sad, then. It was that look that he got at the doctor's office, or when he talked real quiet on the phone. His face deflated like a basketball. He opened his mouth to say something, but then closed it, then opened it again, and then shut it tight.

Finally, he opened his mouth and five words fell out:

Time

is

all

we

got.

11

NANA PARKED THE BOAT ON AN OLD, ABANDONED DOCK. OWLS swirled overhead as we loaded into her station wagon. I jumped in, and almost shut my wing in the door. As I struggled with my seatbelt, she took off down the road. Trees flew by my window.

"Where are we going?"

"Back to OMSI. There are police crawling all over the place looking for you. We need to show them you're okay. There's an ambulance. They'll fix that." She pointed at my arm. "It stopped bleeding, right?"

"Right."

"Good. OMSI first." She pulled out her phone and tossed it in my lap. "Call your father."

"We can't go back to OMSI," I said. "It's not just the police. There's—"

"Gwyn. Call your Father. He's worried about you."

The last time I saw him was right before I flew through a window. I remember how his face twisted as the ball of light slammed into me. She was right. He had to be freaking out. I pulled at the wrap around my arm. "Does he know about my wings?"

Nana stared at the road ahead, flexing her jaw. "Not yet." She scratched her neck, then slowly shook her head. "And don't tell him."

"Don't tell him?" I looked back at my wings, which I had barely stuffed into the car. I ruffled them against the seat. "How am I not going to tell him? They're a little bit obvious."

She ignored the question. "Your father. His research. I should have...I didn't even think. We can't—"

She stopped at the stop sign, then suddenly swerved to the right.

"Where are we going?"

"Road trip. To the hospital. Where I used to work. I know people."

"Won't the police find out?"

"Yes. I want them to. They'll ask you questions, but I'm not worried about that. We can deal with them. And we'll have help at East Memorial."

"Am I going to be okay?"

For just a moment, a slice of sadness slipped onto her face, but it was gone before I took my next breath.

"You'll probably need stitches," she said. "And antibiotics. I'm not going to pull off that fabric. We'll need to soak it first so it doesn't tear. It looks disgusting, by the way, probably crawling with disease. Did you fall into the river?"

"More like I was pushed—"

"You have the heart of a boar, my dear. Pure courage. We'll get to East Memorial. Dr. Mamau will examine you. And he'll buy us some more time, too."

"Time for what?"

Nana stared at the road ahead. "Time to work out a better plan."

"Road Trip!" Mom yelled, tossing my backpack on the floor.

"Where are we going?" I asked.

"To the ocean," Mom said. "I need to get out of here. I need to see the sea. Feel the waves."

"But I have school tomorrow."

"You do."

"And math homework."

"Bring it with."

"It's 4PM."

"Better hurry up then. I want to see the sunset."

"And eat salt water taffy?"

"And dig my toes in the sand."

I grabbed my hoodie. "Is Dad coming with us too?"

"If he gets here in the next five minutes. Otherwise, he's got the night off and we have the ocean."

12

"DAD!"

"Gwyn! Where are you? I've been looking for you everywhere! Are you okay?"

I pushed the phone closer to my ear. "Yes! I'm fine. Nana's got me."

"Nana – how?" There was a click on the line, then someone swore. Dad never swears.

"Dad? Are you okay?"

"Yes! Where are you?"

His voice sounded strange. Like he'd been crying or yelling. Or both.

"Is someone else there?" I could swear I heard someone else breathing. Dad was never that loud.

The line went quiet. "No," Dad said. "No. Just me. Everyone else is outside. I'm at OMSI. We've been searching for you everywhere for hours. What happened? I thought you were hurt. Are you okay? Where are you?"

He sounded weird, but I guess it must have been an impossible day for him too. I mean, last thing he knew, I was in the

Willamette River. Sinking. Like a wet rock. Covered in water. Probably dead and stuff after flying through that window. "We are on our way to the hospital."

"Are you okay?"

"Yes, I'm fine!"

The line rustled again, and I heard a low murmur on the other side of the line. I pushed the phone even closer.

"Okay, okay," Dad said. "Where are you going?"

It's like he wasn't even listening to me. "East Memorial."

"Wait. What? Hospital? Why? You said you were fine. Are you okay?"

"Dad! You've asked me that like eighty times! I'm fine. I just hurt my arm."

"Gwyn. You flew through a window. I'm your dad. I get to ask you if you're okay."

I took a breath. He was just worried about me. Apparently, a giant ball of light plowing into me and shoving me through a window was all it took to get my dad's attention.

"I'll see you at East Memorial," he said. "Wait for me. Don't talk to anyone. I can't believe you climbed that T-Rex."

"I had to! That ball of light—"

"That's enough. I'll see you there."

The phone clicked, and I stared down at the black plastic in my hands. "He doesn't even care. I could be dripping blood. A full-on zombie. It wouldn't matter. He just wants me to not be in trouble."

Nana patted my leg. "He cares, honey. He's just not good at it. He's been like that since he was your age. All vinegar and no sugar. I used to think it was my fault, but then I realized that's just him. He has a scientific mind."

"And no heart," I said.

"His heart just beats in his head."

"That doesn't make any sense."

"It will."

"Mom was better at this stuff."

Nana sighed really deep. "She was. It's like his feet are welded to the ground, and she's floating in the stars."

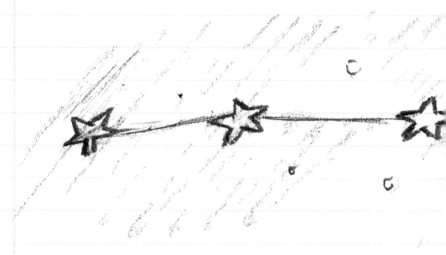

"What's that one?" I asked.

Mom had convinced Dad to bring the sleeping bags to the backyard, without the tent. She wanted to see the stars.

"That is Ursa Major," Dad said. "Commonly known as the Big Dipper."

"Come on, Dad. I was asking Mom. She's the one who knows the stories."

Dad rolled his eyes and Mom laughed her big, rumbling laugh. "Be kind, or you'll end up like Arthur."

"King Arthur?" I asked. "I'd love to be a king. I'd live in a castle."

Dad smirked. "Do you know how

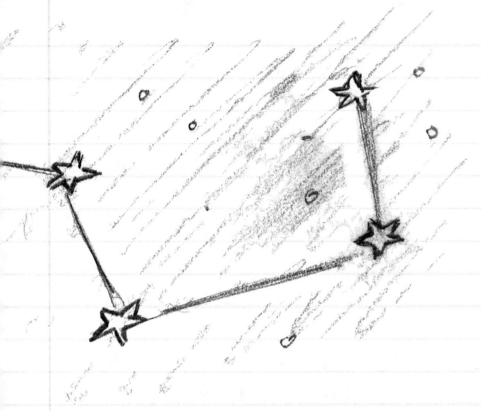

expensive it is to maintain a castle?

"But worth it," Mom said.

"Totally," I added.

Mom pointed up. "The Big Dipper is King Arthur's Chariot, though it's had many other names. Long ago, his chariot represented home. You'd see the Big Dipper, and you'd remember that no matter where you were, no matter how big the sky or how dark the night, a light was burning for you back at home."

Mom turned her face away from the stars and looked over toward me. Her eyes were shining. "Gwyn, you're going to meet many wild and wonderful things in your life, and people are going to both fail you and forgive you. But if you ever can't see the light, you gotta be that light, do you hear me? You gotta shine."

"Brighter than the sun?" I asked.

"Brighter than the stars," Dad said.

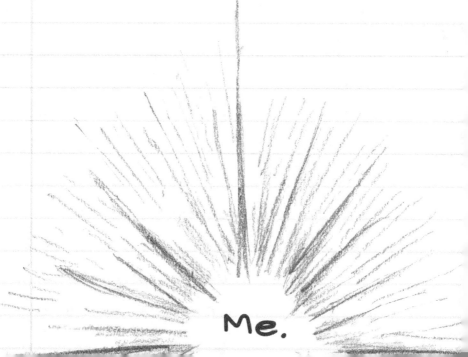

Me.

13

DR. MAMAU WAS SHORT, TAN, AND SEEMED VERY, VERY STRANGE.
I said hi, but he didn't say a thing. He just pulled up a stool,
patted the hospital bed, and I jumped up on it. He soaked my
bandage in some sticky stuff, unwrapped my arm, and
proceeded to wash, clean, and meticulously stitch and bandage
up the cut before he spoke a single word.

When the last stitch was in, he set down the needle, and
finally spoke.

"He has wings," he said.

"He does," Nana replied.

"I do."

"That is unexpected," he said.

"It isn't," Nana said.

"It was for me!"

"You did not tell him?" he asked.

"Not exactly," Nana said.

"Tell me what?"

"You have wings," he said.

"He does," Nana added.

"I know that!"

Dr. Mamau snapped off his gloves. "Keep that clean. Remove the stitches in ten days. I will find the clothes."

Nana pointed at my wings. "He'll need Arthur's Mantle."

Dr. Mamau hopped down from his stool. "It is his birthright. It is his due."

"Who are you?" I asked.

He looked up at me from under his hairy brow. "Your people have words for us. We like very few of them. Your grandmother calls me Dr. Mamau. That will do." He turned back to Nana. "Your police are here. And others. I would not trust them. Monsters. I will find the clothes." He shuffled out of the room.

I pulled the blanket back over me, but my wings fluffed out. "Don't let them in here! Close the door! What are we going to say?"

"You have a concussion." Her purse flew out and bonked me right in the head.

"Ow!" I rubbed my head. My hair was still wet. "What are you doing?"

"You're confused. Tired. Scared. I'll handle the rest."

"I *am* confused. You didn't have to hit me in the head." I rubbed the bump on my forehead as Nana rummaged around in her purse. "I already crashed through a window."

"Hush now. Think about what I said. And don't talk. Unless you have to. Which you don't."

It was hard to think about anything. Maybe I did have a concussion. My brain was mush. Confused, tired, scared – that didn't even begin to describe how I felt. And I had to explain that to the police. Again.

My chin trembled, and I snapped my mouth shut. Police. The last time I talked to the police was when Jaiden and I got in trouble for...well...walking outside. We were on our way back to my house from Jules' place. Jaiden was going to spend the night. It was late, but not too late. The cop car pulled up beside us, and two policemen jumped out.

"What are you two up to?" one said, adjusting his cap.

Something froze in my stomach. My mind stuck. Spun around in circles. I stared at the ground. We weren't up to anything. We were walking. Was that what he wanted to know? My mouth hung open, but no words came out.

Luckily Jaiden's a talker. His long black hair fell in his face as he started in. "We're on our way to Gwyn's house—"

The other cop crossed in front of the car and stood next to me. "It's a little late, isn't it, boys? To be out walking?"

It was nine o'clock. I wanted to shout, but the words wouldn't come. I tried to clear my throat, but I didn't want to make a noise. Jaiden just smiled even bigger. "Gwyn's Dad was supposed to pick us up, but he forgot. That's Gwyn. My name is Jaiden—"

The policeman with the cap braced his hands on his hips. My breath caught. Stuck. "Please take your hands out of your pockets, son. Slowly."

The other policeman dropped his hand to his belt. My chin trembled.

Jaiden slowly pulled his hands out of his pockets, and left his palms up. "My last name is Jackson. Jaiden Jackson. My mom is the DA. Do you know her? You probably know her. She works with the police a lot."

The cop took a swift step back and smiled. "Jackson, huh? That's great. Good lady. You're her kid? Haven't seen you around."

"Around the courthouse? Yeah. That would be weird. We usually play basketball instead."

The policeman laughed, a sudden burst of sound that jolted through me. He turned back toward his car door. "Tell your mom we said hi. And get back home. It's too late to be outside hanging around."

"Gotcha. Thanks, guys," Jaiden said.

I listened as the car doors slammed. I watched as the car pulled away from the curb. I ran my hand slowly over my forehead. My fingers shook.

"You okay, Gwyn?"

"Yeah," I whispered, cleared my throat, and said it again. "Yeah." I looked over at Jaiden. He was watching the car drive away. "How'd you do that?"

He looked away for a second longer, then turned back toward me. "Do what?"

"That." I pointed at the lights fading down the street. "All of it. The words. The talking. I froze. I couldn't speak."

"Dad taught me. Drilled it in. Hijo, say your name. Your dad didn't teach you?"

I shook my head. Not a chance. I'd barely even seen Dad that week, much less talked to him.

"Okay," Jaiden said. "Here's the deal. You don't move unless they tell you to. You don't speak unless they ask you to. And, first chance you get, you say your name. So they know who you are. And, if you can, you always say my mom's name. She knows everybody, and they won't mess with her. Got it? Don't move. Say your name."

"Why do you say your name?"

Jaiden stared at me, his lips pursed into a hard line. "So they know who you are. That you're a real person. And then maybe they won't shoot you."

His words stuck in my head. *Don't move. Say your name.* So they won't shoot you. I thought of those words every time I saw a policeman after that, and they ran back through my mind as the door shot open.

I pulled the blanket up around me, but it was just Dr. Mamau. He held a pile of clothes out to me.

"That was fast," I said, taking the clothes from his very hairy hands.

"They are not real," he said.

Weird. They felt real. They felt like clothes. What did not-clothes feel like?

"But it does not matter," he added. "They will suit until the time is right. Place the mantle first."

I searched through the pile of not-clothes. "I don't see a mantle. What even is a mantle?"

Nana reached into the pile and pulled out a long strip of dark leather. "Did you magick it?" she asked.

"As much as I could," Dr. Mamau said. "It is not all aligned. Taliesin destroyed many threads. I know you loved him, but I do not. His magic is so human."

"Um," I started, but Dr. Mamau was already on his way out the door. Nana huffed and started wrapping the leather around my chest, pulling my wings in against my shoulders.

"If this is going to work, you will need to suspend your disbelief—" Nana stopped, pulled the leather tighter, and my wings tucked in closer to my back. "Actually, don't suspend your belief. Believe. I want you to believe. I want you to think, in a very straightforward way, that everything your mom ever told you is real. Do you understand? I want you to believe that all the stories are true."

I thought back to the Mabinogion, to all the stories she had told me from Welsh mythology. "Brân?"

Nana wrapped the strap around again. "Yes."

"Arthur?"

She pulled the strap under my arm. "Yes."

"Then that means—"

"Yes." She tucked the strap in, and stepped back. "Yes to everything."

My wings tingled, slipping and sliding underneath the leather. As I watched, the dark strap faded to white – just like a bandage – and my wings pulled in even tighter. "What's happening?" I asked.

"They're shrinking."

"Permanently?"

"No. You'll be able to use them when you need them. Just make sure you—"

A knock on the door. Hard.

"One moment—" Nana said.

"They're coming!" Dr. Mamau said. "Check outside."

Nana threw the sweatpants at me, and I pulled them on quickly. She tossed the shirt to me and ran to the window. I accidentally dropped it, squeaked loudly, covered my mouth, grabbed it, and pulled it over my head.

"We have to go!" Nana said, and yelled out the door: "Come in!"

I looked out the window, and saw a black car in the parking lot, with several men jumping out. One of them looked familiar – gray hair, gray suit, and so tall. It looked like Wythe. Kai's Dad. I rubbed my eyes. I'd seen him at OMSI too. Why was my Dad's boss at the hospital? And who were all those men with him?

"Take him out the back," Dr. Mamau said, passing Nana a bag.

"Thank you," she said, catching his eye. "Truly."

She hurried me down the hall. "Head toward the exit. I'll meet you at the car."

"Where are you going?"

"To slow them down."

Gwyn Wylde's Medical Record

Pre-existing Conditions
* Chicken Pox
* Parental Loss
* Acne
* Emotional Instability
* Anxiety
* Clinical Depression
* Right arm: 5 stitches
* Wings

Prescriptions
* Duloxetine for anxiety
* Azelaic Acid for acne
* Mantle for wings

14

NANA IS BOTH INCREDIBLE AND ABSOLUTELY EXASPERATING. AFTER
diving into the car, peeling out of the parking lot, and shouting
at the unexpected traffic, she went quiet. Real quiet.

"Just close your eyes, Gwyn, I need to think."

I settled my head against the window, a thousand questions
running through my head. There's no way I would ever fall
asleep with all that mental noise.

I was out like a light.

Part of me wondered if that was bad, and I had a concussion, and I was going to wake up dead, but the other part of me
was already asleep.

I dreamed I was walking into Oaks Park with Jules and
Jaiden. Nana had dropped us off, mumbling about parking and
capitalism. I knew it was a dream because she handed us a pile
of money before she drove away. That would never happen in
real life.

We bought ride bracelets and headed for the concession
stand. Jules ordered the rainbow sherbet cotton candy with Pop
Rocks sprinkles and Nerds sauce. I could hear the Pop Rocks
sizzling. Jaiden tried the strawberries and whipped cream

cotton candy with a waffle on top. But that wasn't all! there was an entire waffle cone inside – with raspberry ice cream. It looked incredible. I picked out the taco supreme cotton candy with extra jalapeños. It sounded strangely good in my dream.

"That looks unbelievable," Jaiden said, finishing off his waffle. His cotton candy was dripping with strawberries.

"You should have gone for the sherbet," Jules added, Pop Rocks exploding with each word.

"You just wish you ordered this one," I said, covering it in mango sauce. I started chowing down before the cotton candy deflated.

It was sweet and spicy and so very hot!

My mouth was on fire, so we each downed cherry slushies while choosing which rides we were going to tackle that day. The answer: all of them.

Don't worry. This isn't one of those dreams where you eat a bunch of food and get sick and barf everywhere and regret your decisions. No way. This dream was awesome.

We got in line for Project Adrenaline – this super sweet pink coaster that we rode every summer. When we got to the front of the line, though, they were handing out wings.

Jules put green ones on, and Jaiden strapped on a pair of purple. The wings stuck in Jaiden's hair, so he whipped out his rubber band and swirled his dark hair up on top of his head like an ice cream cone. I laughed and waved the attendant away. "I got this," I said. My wings popped out, shining white in the morning sun.

"Let's do this!" Jaiden yelled. He ran up the roller coaster tracks and without a second thought, he jumped off the side, zooming into the sky and then dive-bombing the cotton candy stand.

"Ready?" I asked Jules.

"Ready," she said.

We ran up the roller coaster together. I could already feel

my wings slicing through the air. She jumped, a scream of laughter in the air, still popping with joy.

I stood at the top, watching them fly. Jaiden grabbed the darts from the balloon stand and popped eight balloons. The attendant tossed him a giant red bear. It sprouted wings and took flight beside him, and they rained down candy on the people at the hot dog stand. Meanwhile, Jules had on skates, and was rollerskating along the rooftops, scaring the pigeons and seagulls, tossing beach balls into the sky. Her red hair bounced into her face, and she pushed it away.

It was wild and wonderful. I stretched out my wings ready to dive—

And then I woke up.

Isn't that how dreams go? Right when you're on the verge of doing something really cool, you wake up and you're in your Nana's car and she's mumbling about the Mabinogian, an old Welsh book your mom used to love.

In a better world, I would have gotten to jump off that roller coaster. But in this world, I still had wings.

Right? Or was that all a dream within a dream?

I wiggled my shoulders, and I could still feel them behind me. Wings. My wings. Yes! Life was weird, but incredibly awesome.

Well, except for the bad stuff. Like Wythe and the weird guys chasing us, and dad freaking out, and we hadn't even talked to the cops yet.

But besides all that, everything was pretty cool.

I rubbed my eyes, wishing I had actually eaten that cotton candy, or at least had a peanut butter and jelly sandwich. I was absolutely starving. But still tired. Exhausted. I couldn't wait to drop into bed. But we had people to talk to. Dad. The cops. OMSI. I sighed, remembering the feel of the T-Rex underneath my sneakers. Food, then phone calls, then bed.

When we got there, the cabin was lit up – every single light in the house was on.

"Who's here?" I asked.

Nana parked the car and turned off the engine. Her eyes narrowed. "I don't see your Dad's car."

I shook my head, watching the front windows. "He wouldn't be here yet. He drives slower than a grandma. Well, not you. Slower than a normal grandma."

"I'm normal enough," Nana said. I almost laughed but she had her serious look on. She pulled the keys out of the ignition and shoved them in her purse. "Loosen the mantle. It will free up your wings in case you need to get out of here like a speeding frog.

I tugged the strap loose and started to take off my shirt.

"You can leave that on. It's not real."

"What does that even mean?"

Nana pointed at my back. "Your wings will pop right through it. The shirt won't tear."

"Wow. Okay. Cool. And I won't have to look for a new shirt every time I Incredible Hulk."

"You can thank Arthur for that."

"Which Arthur?"

Nana turned and gave me a look.

"What?" I said.

"Arthur," she repeated. "*The* Arthur."

I swallowed carefully. "The King?"

Nana smiled, the corner of her mouth sneaking upward. "He loved to call himself that. Very regal. Important. But not many other people did."

I looked at Nana, then looked at her living room window, then looked back at Nana again. I knew we didn't have time, but I couldn't help myself. "Arthur is real?"

"*Was* real," Nana said. She patted my leg gently. "Just remember what I said. It will make things easier. Instead of assuming the stories can't be true, assume they are real. Expect anything."

"So..." My mind spun around the idea, and the words stuck. Arthur was real. That means... "Morgan Le Fay?"

"Think bigger."

"Fairies?"

"Bigger."

"Dragons?"

"There we go. And yes, there could be a dragon inside my house right now."

"And you talk to birds?"

"And your shirt isn't real. Got it?"

I shook my head. "No. No, I don't got it. I mean, I won't have to Incredible Hulk anymore, and I'm not green, but I've still got giant wings shooting out of my back. It's unbelievable. I'll always be hiding them. I'll never be able to take off my shirt in public—"

"Is that going to be a big problem?"

I snorted, then sighed. Really big.

"I'm sorry, honey."

"I know. It's just. Mom..." I trailed away. I swear I saw a flicker of movement in the living room.

"But how do they make you feel?"

"Huh?"

"The wings," Nana said. Her eyes were glued to the front window. "How do they really make you feel?"

I paused, then looked back at Nana. That smile was still on her face. I couldn't help but smile too.

"Fine. Okay. They're pretty cool."

Nana nodded her head and turned back toward the house, her purse clasped to her side.

I thought about what the wings meant. I wanted to think about the cool stuff, but all I could think of was the problems. People could have wings in stories and in dreams. Heck, you could jump off a rollercoaster in the Wonderful World of Slumberland. But having them in real life was a totally different situation. I mean, how would I take care of them? Did I have to preen my feathers? Was I going to grow a beak? And what about the T-Rex? And the cops? "Things are going to get really complicated."

"That's an understatement," Nana said. "Someone's inside." I flicked my eyes back to the window. She put her purse up on her shoulder, flipped the car lights back on, and stared up at the house. The bright lights shone into the windows and lit up the yard.

If anyone was in there, they knew we were outside now. Apparently we weren't going for stealthy.

"What's the plan?" I asked, opening my car door.

"Them," she said and pointed up.

I jumped out of the car and my wings spread as I looked up. The trees rustled, then exploded down toward the house. Owls – swirling everywhere. I fell back against the car. They spun and twirled through the air. I'd never seen so many owls before in my life. They were like a swarm of bees, like a golden arrow, like a...big bunch of birds. It was unreal. I thought she only had one owl, but there they were, and—

I hit the floor as they dive-bombed the house, wings and feathers sliding along windows, flanking the side of the house, and pushing open the doors. The house rumbled, vibrated and shook. Then, a loud scream, something crashed to the ground, and the front door shot open. Out ran my best friends, Jules and Jaiden, and – for some weird reason – Kai.

"Kids," Nana said. "Sounds like they broke something. Better not be my one of my ceramics." Nana had a gigantic collection of ceramic birds. It made more sense once I thought about the owls, but it was still kind of weird, and just the tiniest bit creepy too. So many birds. They were always watching you. "Come on," Nana said. "Let's go inside." The owls spun around the cabin one more time, wings breaking through the evening air, and then flew back into the trees, disappearing into the darkness.

Jaiden, Jules and Kai were staring at the car, eyes squinting into the headlights. Nana flipped off the lights, and Jules rubbed her eyes, then a big smile broke onto her face. I pulled my wings in tight and shoved my hands in my pockets.

"What are you guys doing here?" I asked.

Jaiden laughed. "Wylde! I can't believe you're alive! That was wicked. Totally awesome! Increíble!"

Jules nodded. "Seriously. I thought you were dead. Kai said you'd be okay, though."

I looked over at Kai, but he was already turning, walking back into the house.

I climbed the stairs to Jules and Jaiden. "How'd you guys get here?"

"Bus," Jaiden said.

"And so much walking," Jules added.

Jaiden threw an arm around my shoulders and then punched me in the gut. I fell backwards, elaborately faking pain to get him off me. He had almost touched my wings.

"Alright, you kids," Nana said. "Enough of that. Get on inside. Do your parents know where you are?"

Jules avoided Nana's eyes, clicking her prosthesis against the porch rail. "We said you'd text them. I hope that's okay. Will you text them?"

"Kai!" she yelled. "Did you talk to your dad?"

"No," Kai yelled back. "He doesn't care where I am."

"Good," Nana said. She huffed and headed into the house. "We don't need to talk to him again." She was stomping, but she was also digging back in her purse, so I thought we'd be okay. Then I heard her yelling again. "Jaiden! Jules! You get in here."

Jaiden and Jules followed her into the house, heads hanging.

"Are those my birds?" she asked. I followed them through the doorway and saw the scattered remains of several ceramic birds lying on the floor. "What happened in here? Some kind of ceramic tsunami?"

"Those owls were attacking us!" Jaiden said.

Nana stared him down, and he lowered his head.

"Sorry," he said.

"Sorry," Jules added.

"You threw my birds?" Nana asked. I glanced up at her face. She didn't look all mad. She looked...it couldn't be right, but I swear...I think she looked proud.

"Sorry," they both said.

"Clean them up, and I'll text your parents." She pounded her way back to her bedroom and slammed the door behind her.

I sat down on the couch, sinking in and pushing back, as Kai reappeared at the kitchen door.

"Where are your wings?" he asked.

Nana never told me stories. She told me facts. About birds, about rainforests, about the world, and the way it was and the way it should be. For example, before I was 4, I knew that the Amazon rainforest is the largest tropical rainforest in the entire world. I knew there are two types of forests: Tropical and Temperate. I knew that the Amazon Rainforest is the home of a large number of indigenous tribes and peoples. That's not all. Because of my

Nana, I also
knew that
colonialism,
capitalism,
and
corporations
(the 3 C's)
had destroyed
those indigenous
peoples, cultures
and languages.
They destroyed their way of
life, as well as the places they called
home. The indigenous peoples
used to travel all over the
rainforest, but they got trapped in
these tiny little pockets of land.
She told me that story while we
were walking through Forest Park.
It was a systemic problem from
the Amazon rainforest, all
the way to Portland.

"This forest was the ancestral home of so many tribes for over 10,000 years," Nana said. "Now, it has a zoo and a rose garden.

"We have to look at what happened and what keeps happening, over and over again. We need to **Break** those patterns. **Learn** from our mistakes and heartbreaks. Protest. Fight. It ain't all a kettle of donkeys."

I never understood the thing about the donkeys, but I got what she was trying to say, about standing up and fighting. So, when the **Black Lives Matter** protests started, I got out my markers, too. She told me to never bow down to the system.

In fact, she taught me those words before I even knew what the system was. She thought the world was stupid, mean, and really unfair. She wanted me to get out there and change it.

"**Fight the power**," she said.

I didn't want to fight. Honestly, I wanted the world to not be so terrible so I could just play video games and basketball with my friends and not be scared of dying. Why did we always have to be fighting?

Nana, though, she'd fight anybody. Dad said she was different when she was younger, but something happened that changed her mind about things. She doesn't think the world is so good anymore. She thinks we need to make it that way.

15

"WHAT? WINGS? THAT'S WEIRD. NO," I MUMBLED, SCOOTING
further back into the couch.

"Your wings," Jules said, plopping down next to me.

Jaiden smiled as he sat on the arm of the chair. "We know
you have them."

"I don't have wings."

Jules poked my shoulder, and I shifted away. "Did you lose
them? Like your glasses?"

"You mean these glasses?" Jaiden asked.

He dangled them in the air, but I grabbed them out of his
hands and pushed them onto my nose where they belonged.
"You guys are being weird," I said.

"You are the one being all extraño. We saw your wings in
the video. We didn't post that part, but they were totally there.
Sus alas!"

"Big white wings," Jules said.

This was getting out of hand. I shook my head. "I can't
believe you posted that video on your YouTube channel!"

"We didn't put up the whole thing," Jaiden said. "Just the

cool part. It already has some many likes! You totally sunk that dare and ran up the dinosaur!"

"Yeah. The dare. I did, didn't I?" I laughed, remembering the bet. "I totally rode that dinosaur! Where are my tacos?"

Kai took a step closer. "You're avoiding the question," he said.

"It's a stupid question," I replied, shifting to the side against my hidden wings. "I don't have wings. People don't have wings. That's not a thing."

"Really?" Jules asked. "Then what's that?"

I looked down. She was pointing to a feather behind me on the couch.

"That's a feather," I said. "Because pillows. With feathers in them. Nana loves pillows."

She grabbed the feather and pulled hard.

"Ow!" I said, and my wing whipped out and smacked her. She fell into the arm of the couch, and I pulled my wing back in. "Sorry – I didn't mean to—"

It was too late. She held the feather up in her hand.

"Yes," she whispered.

I took a deep breath, then let it out slowly. "Yes," I said.

"So cool!" Jaiden yelled.

"Okay," Jules said. "Let's see them."

Part of me wanted to just lay back on the couch. Close my eyes. Go to sleep, and stay that way for a long time. But the other part of me, well, maybe it wanted to show off. Just a little bit. I mean, it had been a long day. And Jaiden was right – my wings were pretty cool.

I pushed up off the couch and walked to the middle of the living room. Jules peered up at me, pushing the curls out of her face. Jaiden drum-rolled on the chair, his hands beating against the broken leather seat.

"And now," he said, "For your viewing pleasure—"

"Knock it off," I said, shaking out my arms.

"Today only," he continued. "Straight down from the sky and into your Nana's living room, the one, the only, WYYYYLDE!"

I bowed my head, holding in the laugh, and stretched my arms to the ceiling. The wings lifted up and the feathers spilled down.

"Amazing," Jules whispered.

"Awesome," Jaiden said.

"Get your Nana," Kai said.

I looked over at him. He stood in the doorway, eyes intense, no trace of a smile on his face.

"Why?"

"We need to talk."

I hate **talking**. After Mom died, everyone wanted to **talk**. My teachers. My therapist. My friends. Talk, talk, talk, talk. Everyone except Dad. He could go a whole week without talking to me. I mean,

Let's talk!

he'd tell me to **do** things like **"Take out the trash"** or **"Get in the car"** or **"Put your shoes on!"** But he

. . .

wouldn't say anything that really **mattered**, you know? He barely even looked at me across the kitchen table. I swear, one day, I had my tongue sticking out for like an hour, sliding back and forth, until it was so dried out I had to get a drink of water. He told me to wash the dishes.

In the beginning, when we went to therapy together, Geneva would ask him questions about how he was feeling. It was so weird and wrong. He was super scientific about it. Everything was about **processing**.

He was **processing** Mom's death. He was **considering** his feelings. He was **developing** a new approach. He was always thinking. Mom was in his head, but not in his heart.

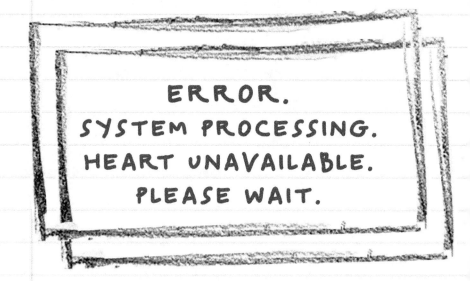

ERROR.
SYSTEM PROCESSING.
HEART UNAVAILABLE.
PLEASE WAIT.

The real Mom,

the Mom that I loved, she wouldn't live in there. Processing? Science? Are you kidding? Now way. Not even. She'd find it too intense, too stuffy, too **boring**. She'd break all those processors. Stop all that thinking. Take me to the ocean or for ice cream on a Wednesday morning.

She was the light and the fire. The stories. The words. She didn't think. She didn't have to.

She lived.

16

I HEADED TO THE KITCHEN FIRST – THEY COULDN'T STOP ME. IF they were going to keep dragging things out, setting me up like a sideshow, I needed to get myself something to eat. I was starving.

And maybe all that hunger and exhaustion was making me just a little bit sassy. Maybe. Probably not. But maybe.

I pulled the peanut butter and jelly out of the fridge and set it on the counter, flipped open the breadbox – with a flock of birds painted across it – and took out the bread. I grabbed an eagle plate from the cabinet.

Honestly, I have no memory of actually making that sandwich. It was like I was on autopilot. Before I knew it, the peanut butter was squished on, the jelly was slathered in, and I was pushing the pieces together.

Heaven – that first bite was perfection.

No matter how much peanut butter and jelly I eat, I could always eat more. Which is good, because PB&J is about half my diet. Not just lunch, but breakfast, snacks, and dinner too.

I usually make my own lunch, but I didn't that day, because of the field trip. I saw Dad making his own lunch in the kitchen, and I just assumed he was making mine too. Stupid assumption, right?

I guess he thinks I don't need to eat anymore either.

The whole situation was messed up. I scarfed that PB&J, and I was still hungry. If Dad was going to keep shutting me out, forgetting that I needed to eat, or that I even existed, well, I would probably need to take a cooking class. I'm pretty sure my nutritional needs were not being met. I wanted to dunk my face in a salad bar – or at least a bucket of apples.

I rubbed my eyes. Longest day ever, and I didn't see it ending soon.

"You okay?"

Jules stood in the doorway, her hand clenching the feather.

"Yeah," I said, blinking away the smudginess. "Yes!"

"Really?" she asked.

She wasn't looking at me – she was smoothing down that feather – but I knew she was waiting, like she does. After all this time, she's got me pretty figured out.

"Just hungry. And tired. It's a lot, you know?"

"It is." She slowly twirled the feather in her hand. "What'd your dad say?"

"Haven't seen him yet."

"Really? Wow. He's gonna freak out. It's like the science of im-possibility."

"Yeah," I said, pulling out another slice of bread. "He was talking to the cops all day and looking for me. He was pretty mad on the phone."

"Kai said it's...complicated."

"Kai knows a lot more than I do. I'll get Nana. We'll figure out what's up with Dad, and, you know, my wings."

She tucked the feather into her pocket.

"Yeah," she said. "Hopefully your dad chills out. He's always cool in school. Well, not cool. Nerdy. But cool."

"Just not with me."

She nodded. I stared down at the slice of bread in my hand. She'd seen Dad do the switch. He couldn't hide it from her. She paid attention.

"I'll get Nana," I said, stuffing the bread in my mouth. Carbs first. Family second.

I opened the door and headed up the stairs, trying to not look up. I knew what I'd see. I had those walls memorized. They were lined with all the pictures from Before. When we took pictures. Before. When we smiled and laughed. Before. When we came to Nana's house on the weekends and swam in the river. Before. When we were a family.

Now what are we? Just a pile of people seeing each other on birthdays and holidays. Just a lot of silence and eating, all that food Nana drops into me, because Dad won't feed me and what else can we do anyway? We can't talk about the things that matter. We can't love each other big enough or see each other bright enough.

We don't shine anymore.

Mom used to say that was the thing about love. It shined. It bounced off your heart and reflected back to the world. You could tell when people loved each other because it made the room brighter.

I hadn't seen that in a long time. Not since the day she left her hospital bed. The moment she closed her eyes for the final time, I had to close mine too. The light was so bright I could barely see.

When I opened them back up, she was gone. And it was dark. Stayed that way.

I raised my hand to knock on Nana's door, but heard a muffled sniffling sound. My hand froze next to the handle. The sniffling went on. I knocked gently and it stopped.

"Come in," Nana said.

I opened the door slowly. She was sitting on the bed, wiping her eyes.

Crying. I didn't even know she could. She never did when Mom was dying. She did everything else but that.

"Are you okay?" I asked.

"Yes," she said. "It snuck up on me."

"What did?"

"Sadness. Sometimes, it pulls the threads of me, and I come unravelled. I'll be fine in a moment."

"What happened?"

"Your mother. She would have loved this. Your wings. Heavens, I just miss her."

"Me too," I said.

But that wasn't right. It was too small. I missed Mom in a big way. She was so much of us, and when she left, there was this empty space. No, a hole. It was a hole. Because I tried to throw things into it to fill the space back in, but it all dropped down into the darkness, and I still felt empty.

Coping strategies, my therapist calls them. Food. Friends. Homework. Basketball. I tried it all. Nothing filled the hole she left.

Depression, my therapist said then. It makes you feel like that. Like you can't get away from the bottom. But so does losing your mom.

"I really miss her," I said.

Nana patted a square of the patchwork quilt, and I sat down beside her on the bed.

"She would be – she is – so proud of you, you know. Your strength. Your kindness. The way you look at the world. It's like you walked out of one of her stories."

I spread my wings out behind us on the bed. "I did."

Nana smiled, and touched my wing gently.

"We need to talk," I said.

"We do," she said.

"We do."

I turned and saw Kai standing at the door. "Seriously, Kai. Don't do that. You're gonna give me a heart attack."

"It's important."

My Coping Strategies

Geneva says "we all use different strategies to cope with stressful or emotional situations." Okay. So. She wants me to list **my** strategies...

Problem-solving strategies

(Geneva says you use these to "actively alleviate stress"):

* Food
* Friends
* Basketball
* Biking
* Running
* Video games
* More food

Emotion-focused strategies

(Geneva says you use these to "deal with the emotions involved with stress"):

* See above?

17

"HE'S COMING."

"Who?" I asked.

"My Dad."

"Who is he?" Nana asked.

"He's Dad's boss," I said slowly.

"He is," Kai said. "But he's something else too."

"What?" I asked.

Kai shrugged, and kept staring at me. I didn't know what to say to him.

Nana stood up, stretching her back. "I should have known. All those men. They were so dirty — practically dripping in glamour. I didn't recognize him. I should have pulled back the veil. What do you know, Kai?"

"I don't know what you are talking about. You will have to explain. But as for your question, I found some notes. In his coat." Kai narrowed his eyes at me. "They had Mr. Wylde – your dad's – name on them. So I started paying attention." He cocked his head. "Mr. Wylde's research – it's not all theoretical. Not like he talks about in class. Energy. Your dad has been researching energy. And he found it. A lot of it. And it behaves in ways he didn't expect. It's breaking the laws."

I scratched my back, trying to get at the spot where my wings met my shoulder blades. It itched like chicken pox. Or wings that were sticking out of my skin. With feathers and stuff. "Laws...like the first law of thermodynamics?"

Kai nodded. "The energy doesn't behave according to our rules. He had a video. On his phone. I saw it. The energy."

I shook my head, and scratched harder. I couldn't get to the right spot. "Why would he have a video of it? What did it look like? And where'd he get it? The energy in the video?"

"That's a lot of questions," Kai said. "Which one would you like me to address? The last one about energy?"

Nana tsked and straightened her dress. "It's not energy, boys. Don't be silly. It's magic. It's life."

"Whatever you want to call it," Kai said, "they've got it. They've got a lot of it."

I scratched my back against the door frame, thinking of how Wythe had glared at me, like I did something wrong. I thought it was just a an adult thing. Running around the museum and whatever. But maybe it was something else. Maybe he knew—

"I should have known," Nana said. "We got lucky with Gwyn. Where are they?"

Nana's phone buzzed inside her purse. We all ignored it. It kept on buzzing.

"*Who* are they?" I asked.

"You know," Nana said. "The story, remember? It's real. All of it. The town – on the other side of the mountain. All those people. They used to be able to fly. It was spellbinding. Magical. Until someone took their spark away. They're the ones. They took them."

Kai scratched the back of his hand, looking at me intently.

"Our dads have them now. The sparks. I think your dad is trying to use them – something about tissue repair. But he has no idea what he is doing. He doesn't know my dad. It's not safe. My dad is just using him. You don't know him like I do."

Nana pulled on her bag. "Where are the sparks?"

"Flicker," Kai said.

I rubbed my face in my hands. "Dad's work. We should get going. It's back downtown by OMSI."

Nana shook her head. "No way. I'm going to free them. Easy as fish. You kids are staying home."

"No, we're not."

I looked back up to see who said that, and I saw Jaiden and Jules behind Kai at the door. "You know, you guys all need to learn to knock."

Jaiden turned around, dramatically knocked on the door, then said: "We're coming with you."

"No," Nana said, in her serious voice. "You kids are not going back in there. It's dangerous. Those men have guns. And terrible attitudes."

Jules pointed at my wings. "Wylde can fly."

"Wylde?" Nana said, looking over at me. "Wylde," she repeated. "Yes. That's your name. The one you earned. Of course it is." She smiled down at me. "You're staying here."

Light beamed through the window, shining over our faces. Kai stared through the glass. "Well, we aren't staying right here," he said.

Nana sighed, long and deep. "Fine. Get in the car." She reached into her purse and tossed me the phone. "And text your dad."

I looked down at Nana's phone. "He left a voicemail."

I pushed play, and his voice played as we headed down to the living room.

"Nana! It's me. Tell Gwyn. There's something I need to do. I can't make it to your house. Tell him I'm sorry. Take care of him, okay? I'm sorry about everything. Whatever happens, don't come back to my work. Stay home. Stay safe. I'll call you in an hour. I love you."

I met Kai the first day of school. Jaiden and I asked him to play basketball on our team with Jules. He said he'd rather watch.

"Come on!" I begged. "Zach's got Rowan, Danny, and Thad. We don't stand a chance."

"If I play," Kai added, "it will significantly lower your odds of winning this game."

"You got this, amigo," Jaiden said, patting him on the back. "All you gotta do is guard Rowan. I'll shoot."

I nudged Jaiden. "More like you'll pass, and I'll shoot."

Jules rolled her eyes at both of us. "More like I'll shoot and you too will talk, talk, talk and wave your arms around a lot, calling for the ball."

Jaiden waved his arms at her.

"Wait," Kai said. "Before anyone does anything with their arms or mouths. Explain to me what happens next. I don't know how to guard."

"That's easy," Jules said. "First off, don't touch him. Just stand in his way. A lot. Run around and make sure no one can pass to him. Make sure he can't shoot and can't pass."

"Get in his way," I repeated.

"Understood," Kai said. "What is your plan? What will you all do?"

"Plan?" Jaiden asked. "We don't plan. It's básquetbol. We just play."

18

I CALLED DAD BACK, BUT HE DIDN'T ANSWER, OF COURSE.

"Hey, Dad! It's me. We're at Nana's house. Some stuff is happening. With your boss. And...me. It's weird. Call me back. Please."

Nana was whispering to Kai, Jaiden and Jules.

"What's the plan?" I asked.

"Owls?" Jaiden asked.

"Owls," Nana whispered.

"That is a terrible plan," Kai whispered back.

Jules squinted over at him. "Did you see her owls?"

"Good point," Kai said.

Really good point. Nana had more owls than I'd ever seen in my entire life. Of course, I'd never even seen an owl until that day, but I guess if you have that many owls, well, your plan is: owls.

We ducked out the back door, and they hooted from the trees, their calls a whirlwind of sound in the darkness. Nana raised her arms and then brought them back down, and the owls followed, crashing through the trees and parting around the house, headed toward the front. We ran behind them, taking the sidewalk to the driveway.

"Stay low," Nana said. We ducked down and more owls swooped over our heads, then shot straight up into the air. Their wings cut into the sky, breaking through the darkness, and then everything was quiet as we made our way up the long gravel drive.

A dog barked nearby, and I scanned the forest. The branches rustled and cracked.

"Stop right there!" someone yelled. A bright light flashed toward us, then another. I squinted into the light. Wythe stared back at me, flashlight in hand. He was standing right in front of Nana's car, with two men in suits.

I scanned the yard – we had nowhere to go. We needed to get to the car, and he blocked it. We were stuck, standing in the driveway, totally exposed.

Wythe looked us up and down. I could feel Nana's phone vibrating in my pocket. Dad has the worst timing.

"We were searching for you kids all over OMSI," he said. His eyes shot over to Kai. "If you would have told me where you were going—"

"I didn't," Kai said.

"You'll regret that," Wythe replied.

"I won't," Kai said quietly.

Wythe moved on. "Nice to see you again, Donna."

"Nope," Nana said. "I don't like you. It's not nice to see you. You're a worm."

He cocked his head to the side. "A worm? Is that really the best you can do?"

Nana smiled – a great, big Sunday smile. "My birds just love squirmy worms." She laughed, and then the air filled with sound.

The owls exploded down from the sky, slamming into Wythe, pushing him away from the car in a barrage of feathers.

He swung his arms in the air, knocking at wings and kicking away biting beaks.

Nana ran for the driver's side door. "Get in the car!"

The birds were unrelenting and unending. They swarmed down from the sky, but parted around us. We ran toward the car. Jaiden got there first, grabbed the back door, and yanked it open. He kicked one of the suits in the shins as Jules jumped in the car. Jaiden spun around and dove in after her, slamming and locking the door.

Kai and I ran to the other side. As Kai pulled open his door, Wythe locked onto his arm. "Get over here!"

I grabbed Wythe's jacket and jerked him away as Kai slammed the back door shut.

The car door burst open, knocking me down to the ground, right next to Wythe, who was now covered in a swarm of owls. "Let's go!" Nana yelled from inside the car.

I scrambled through the gravel toward the door, kicking away Wythe's scrambling hands.

He growled and then roared and reached into his pocket. Suddenly a huge black dog flew through the air and smashed into his chest. One paw clawed at his suit as the dog tore at his arm. The birds took to the sky.

Dog wasn't quite the right word. It was huge – the size of a bear. Maybe it *was* a bear. Its eyes flashed red as it shook Wythe's arm from side to side. I dove out of the way as the dog flung him into the car door, which slammed shut. Wythe groaned and reached for my arm, but the dog lunged and snapped onto his pants leg, then ripped him away from me.

I freaked out. I jumped to my feet, grabbed the door handle, pulled the door open, and was almost in the car when someone slammed into the door, shoving me away from the car and banging the door shut again. I landed on my hands and knees. "Come on!" I yelled. "Just let me get in the stupid car!"

I looked up to see Wythe struggling with the dog. "You're coming with me," he yelled.

"No," I said, "I'm not."

Nana's old car roared to life, and I rolled out of the way and onto my feet. He dove toward me, grabbing a hold of my shirt. The dog clamped down on his legs and I ripped away from Wythe. My shirt tore free suddenly, and he stumbled backward into the car. The car peeled out behind him, and he tumbled forward, headed straight for me again with that flock of birds clawing into him.

Wythe was totally out of his mind. Any normal person would have given up, or tried a new tactic, but he was like a steamroller. No wonder Kai hated him so much. He was the Terminator or the Coyote who wouldn't leave the Roadrunner alone. Straight up evil.

But I knew I was wilder. In fact, I was Wylde!

"Wylde!" I yelled.

Okay, that was a little bit dorky, but I needed it. Long night. I pumped myself up, rolled back my shoulder. Yes! Wylde! I could do anything!

Except fight. I suck at that. Everything except for fighting. I hate fighting.

But I can run. I turned and kicked it into the forest, full on sprinting. He yelled behind me, struggling and crying out, but I didn't turn back. I didn't want to know. I just waved my hands, stretched out my wings, and took to the sky.

He Ain't Coming to Town

I held the stocking out to Mom, the red yarn spilling from my fingers. "Santa Claus isn't real," I told her.

She laughed at me, big and loud, like she'd never heard anything more ridiculous in her whole entire life. "Of course he's real, honey. And don't you dare go believing he's not. You're seven years old. That would cost us way too much money."

I looked up at her face, the way her brown hair fell down to her shoulders. She was setting down her pencil. Maybe she wasn't listening. She probably didn't hear me.

"Jaiden told me. He said he saw his mom put out his presents last year."

"Of course he did. That kid has the imagination of a stick, and not even a big one at that."

"Come on, Mom. Leave him alone."

"You brought him up. I love Jaiden, but he's gonna crash and burn. He's too brave. Bam! He'll punch someone important. It's not his fault. He lives in his body too much. Jules has got a better chance. She can see with more than her eyes."

I didn't know what she was talking about, but I let it go. "Santa, Mom. What about Santa?"

"Red hat? Big white beard?"

I glared at her.

Her eyes twinkled.

I took a deep breath.

She winked at me.

"He's not real, is he?"

Her brow furrowed, and she finally turned to face me completely. "You know, the second you start questioning whether Santa Claus is real, he's not anymore. Not for you. Magic needs belief. It runs on it."

"Like gas?"

"Exactly. If magic is a car, belief is its gas. You don't believe, your car won't work. Or worse yet, it might not even exist. You'll have to take the train, or walk to the North Pole."

"Wait a second. If I don't believe, he won't be real? At all?"

"Not for you he won't. He'll just move onto all the other kids whose magic is still strong. All those kids who still believe in him and his magic."

I looked down at the stocking in my hand, all red and white like Santa's hat. I didn't want to stop believing in Santa. I needed him.

But Jaiden had stuck up for me t recess. I clenched the stocking tight. The other kids were calling me baby.

Mom patted the top of my head. "You know, if you stop believing, I'll have to start buying your presents, and they won't be nearly as good.

I almost dropped the stocking. "So, I won't get the Death Star?"

She rolled her eyes. "Kid, you'll be lucky to get the Tie Fighter."

"Then tell him," I said, shaking the stocking. "Tell him I believe. In all of it. Right now. Call him."

"I will." She nudged me away. "Now get out of here and go hang your stocking back up. And write him that letter. Tell him about the Death Star and the video game. He's got some presents to make."

I paused at the door, looking back at Mom. She was already bent back over her desk. "Are his elves real?" I asked. "The ones that work for him?"

She didn't even look up. "Don't be ridiculous, Gwyn. Elves wouldn't work for that   madman."

19

THE MOON WAS OUT, SHINING DOWN ON THE TREES, AS I FLAPPED
my wings and panted my way over the sprawling forest. Stupid
Wythe. Straight up dumb. And what was the deal with that
dog? Unreal – directly out of a nightmare. It was huge.
Unnatural.

My arms trembled into the wind. I wasn't sure how much
longer I could keep them going. Nana said I could move my
wings without moving my arms too, but I couldn't figure out
how. It all seemed connected, stretching out my shoulders and
arms, but I couldn't raise them on my own – they didn't work
that way.

I was tired. So tired.

And hungry. Why didn't I make more PB&Js? Or tacos. With
guacamole. Jaiden seriously owed me.

I searched the road for the flash of Nana's brake lights, but
saw nothing except a long line of asphalt snaking through the
forest. Maybe Nana had turned off her lights so they couldn't
find her. I pumped my wings over and over. They would be
okay – they had Nana's owls and were already on their way.
Jaiden would probably even take a nap in the car, while Kai

explained what was going on. I wished I was there for that explanation, but I'd just have to meet them at Flicker.

If I could find it.

Route 30. If I could get there, I could take that right into town and straight down toward Flicker. Then everything would be fine.

But I never paid attention on the winding roads through the forest. Sure, we'd just driven to the cabin, but I was half asleep on our drive over. Brain dead. Dreaming about cotton candy and roller coasters. It was all a bunch of twists and turns and everything looked totally different from up—

Wait. What?

I stared down at the road. It was blue. Shimmering – almost shining. Not all the roads. Just one. I shifted in the wind, and the blue road suddenly moved.

No — it wasn't a road. It was a shimmery blue line, curving through the trees, scoring its own path.

I turned and the line curved. Up ahead, it swirled back around the way it started.

I twirled to follow it, and it straightened back out. I'd seen the line before. Over the forest, for just a moment. Before Nana's owl showed up.

Directions. It was giving me directions, like the line on an iPhone. Go this way, Gwyn.

Of all the strange stuff that had happened, blue lines were the weirdest. I had my own magic GPS.

It didn't seem actually possible. I mean, it couldn't be real, could it? I flapped my wings and remembered what Nana had said – just believe. Believe it was all true, and that anything is possible.

In that case, I was going to believe in the Flying Taco Man who served burritos in the sky with a side of PB&J.

I didn't see him magically appear.

Maybe I just needed to believe harder?

I followed the line forward and thought about what to do. I needed to test out my theory – to see if the line was leading me where I really wanted to go. If it took me to Route 30, I could trust it.

The shimmer curved through the forest, and I flapped my wings high above. I felt like a goose, migrating through the sky, soaring, following a line that only I could see.

A flash of black along the line broke the blue shimmer. A dark blur ran beside the line. Sprinting. So fast. What was it? A bear? It looked like a giant – dog.

I banked low and narrowed my eyes. The same dog from the cabin. The one that attacked Wythe. Giant, black, and barreling through the forest, following the line, unswerving, paws tearing into the forest floor.

I slowed, and it slowed, turning onto a road to follow the line, when out of nowhere a car—

"No!" I yelled.

Its head whipped up toward me, and then, almost casually, it kicked its feet and leapt over the car, landed lightly, and crimson eyes flashed back up at me. Paws clawed the ground, and its giant teeth hung from its mouth, glittering in the moonlight. My stomach dropped, and I flew off again.

It followed.

Crap. Not only was I being tailed by my dad's boss and a group of angry businessmen, now I had a demon dog on my tail too, and Nana was nowhere in sight. I needed to get to Flicker and to Dad and get all this figured out, and then I would—

That's when I saw them.

Shining blue in the middle of the darkest night.

Zombies.

Note to self:

I

am having a
very,
very,
very,
bad
day.

20

THEY WERE FAST – CRASHING THROUGH THE FOREST. THEY glowed, just like that line.

I flew in closer to get a look.

Yep. Zombies. Zombies!

Missing arms. Rotting flesh. Blood and guts and other stuff. All blue. Totally gross. And the dog was right on their decomposing feet, nipping at their decaying heels.

I was about to pinch myself, or slap myself, but right then, a branch cracked into my face. SMASH!

And I fell.

I crunched through the trees, arms flailing, wings snagging, hurtling through the sky, until I finally crashed into the ground, legs failing beneath me.

The air was gone – knocked from my lungs. I scrambled onto my knees, pushing my glasses up my nose, and pulling my wings through the brush, gasping. The air slowly cut back into my chest, sharp and hot. I spread out my wings, but leaned down on one hand.

Hey! Cool! My wings worked on their own.

I straightened up and pumped my fist. Awesome.

I laughed as I looked up at the sky, but swallowed the sound as dark red eyes stared into mine.

The demon dog.

I jumped to my feet and took off, arms flapping, speeding up my wings. The forest was too packed! I couldn't off the ground, couldn't get a head start. Trees, bushes everywhere. Too tight. No wing space. Not enough room to take off or spread my wings full out. I could barely run between all those branches.

That dog was hot on my tail, crashing through the forest behind me as I cut and swerved around limbs, branches slicing into my face.

Up ahead the trees cleared and the moonlight broke through into a clearing. I busted out, pounded my feet, lifted my wings, and promptly tripped. Hard.

Dirt went straight into my mouth. I spit it out, rolled to the side, and when I looked up, the demon dog was flying through the air. I opened my mouth to scream, but then he was on me, claws tearing through my shirt. He lunged for my face, opened his gaping maw, and he licked me. Licked me! A great, big, sloppy, wet, demon dog kiss. Slobber dripped down into my eyes.

"Get off me!" I yelled. The bear-dog-monster scrambled off immediately, and I stood up, running my hands over my chest. The tears in my shirt disappeared. My shirt wasn't real. Was the dog real? The demon dog stepped back, panting, tongue lolling out, staring down into my eyes. The dog was real. Very real.

My hands were soaked with drool. I wiped them on my pants as I watched the drool slide out of his mouth. He was *huge*. And he was just standing there, looking at me.

"Sit," I said.

And he sat.

Demon dog was listening to me.

I weighed my options. I could take to the sky – leave demon

dog behind me. Or I could fly low. The dog could follow along. I think it was trying to help me at Nana's cabin – attacking Wythe and everything. It seemed to be a part of all this. The wings, the lines, Wythe. It definitely didn't like Wythe. And it was chasing those zombies—

"Demon dog," I repeated.

It cocked its head. That was too big of a name. Hard to say. "DD," I said.

Ears shot up. I think it liked that name.

"Okay," I said. "DD."

I'd never had a dog before...much less one the size of a bear. Where would it even sleep? Did it sleep? It didn't look like it could slept. But it definitely looked like it ate. A lot. What did it eat? Dog food? Other dogs? People? Entire grocery stores?

It whined, long and loud.

"What is it, boy?" I asked. How did I know it was a boy? It could be a—nope. He was a boy. His head whipped toward the forest, and he whined again.

"What's wrong?"

I shook my head. He couldn't really understand me. DD was a dog. Why was I talking to a dog and expecting it to talk back? That wasn't possible.

Seriously, though, I had wings. If that was possible, why not a smart dog? Nana said it. Believe everything. Still no Flying Taco Man, or randomly appearing guacamole. That would be awesome.

Zombies, though. Those were real too. Ugh.

DD barked at me, loud. His tail thumped the ground.

"Let's go, DD," I said. We had enough of the world to save. I wasn't going to figure out where those zombies went. They'd have to wait until we found Nana. And a giant fire pit to throw them into. Or, like a volcano, or something? Ugh. Zombies.

I ran through the clearing, flapping my wings, and then took to the sky. DD tracked me from the ground, pounding along, and as I rose up above the tree line, the path glowed blue once more in the darkness. I flew above again, and DD ran along on the path.

Just as I was starting to pick up some speed, I saw Camp Friendly Tree. The lodge was lit up, flooding light down onto the cabins. Kids were wandering around the front lawn, and a bonfire lit up the fire ring – a blaze of light shining in the darkness – with a hoard of zombies headed right toward it.

Camp Friendly Tree Hearth Song

Camp Friendly Tree,
we wave a flag for you!
To Frank, Tilly, Tommy,
and the counselors too.
We always have such fun
when we hike and we work
in the dirt and the sun.
Oh, we swim and we bike
and we talk a lot
cuz nothing's better
than the friends we've got.
It's important that we know
that with you, we will grow.
You'll always be our favorite camp

Our Camp Friendly Tree!

21

So many kids. Little campers. We had to get down there. I hit the wind hard with my wings, diving down.

Wait. Kids? Why were there campers in May? I'd been to Camp Friendly Tree every year since Mom died. It's a touchy-feely make new friends camp. It's where I met Jules. It ran during the summer months – and school wasn't even out yet. Why were there all those kids and bonfires? They should be at home.

I zoomed in closer, and realized my mistake. They weren't campers – they were counselors. Training week at Camp Friendly Tree and time to get eaten by zombies.

They had a solid five minutes before the zombies came. Then it was over. Straight horror movie. They wouldn't last more than the commercial break. Camp songs and s'mores weren't gonna stop the undead.

Kumbay-ouch! Ow, my head.

That would be funny if it was Brad. Brad's the worst. Super mean. If a zombie was gonna eat his head, I'd totally let it almost happen. Just enough to freak him out, and maybe make him a better person.

I really am not good in stressful situations. Everyone knows that. And this was turning into a doozy of a day. And doozy is a dumb word. Focus. Focus. Get them inside. Draw away the zombies.

Stop the horror movie.

I sped ahead of the zombies, wings pumping harder than ever. "Come on, DD!" I yelled. He kicked it too – he ran right by the zombies, pausing for just a moment to nip one in the bright blue thigh.

We zoomed ahead and past the tree line, where I pulled up quickly and lowered myself at the edge of the trees. How was I going to get those counselors out of there? They were relaxing around the bonfires, probably arguing about cars or working out or something. Little groups spread out all over the front patio. How could I convince them to get off the lawn? I laughed, then covered my mouth and laughed again.

I couldn't just yell, "Get off my lawn!"

I jumped as DD swished through the bushes beside me. He nudged my hand, and I tried to be cool. I'd never get used to a giant demon dog breathing hot air all over my arms and licking my fingers. I shoved my slobbery hand in my pocket.

DD! That was it.

"Listen, DD," I said. His ears perked up. I hoped he could understand basic commands. "I need you to stay here. Stay. Don't come until I call you. And then, when I point at you, just chase me. Only me. Nobody else. Growl and be super intimidating. Got it?"

His tongue lolled out, and I crossed my fingers and pulled my wings in tight. "Stay," I said. "Stay!" I repeated, then took off for the bonfire.

"Help!" I screamed. "Help! It's a giant bear! With rabies! And bees!"

I ran toward the bonfire, and the counselors shot right to their feet.

"It's gonna eat me!" I ran right into a counselor and grabbed her arm. "Bear! It's gonna eat us! All of us! We got to get out of here right now!"

"What are you talking about?" she asked, shrugging off my arm.

"Sorry," I said. "I didn't mean to grab you...It's just...there's a really big—"

Suddenly, Brad was right up in my face. I could see very inch of his stupid muscles and dumb tank top. "What are you doing here, little creep? It's not time for kids. It's training week. I'm not ready for this yet. Go home. Wait. How'd you get here?"

The girl nudged Brad away. "Give him a break, Brad. Something is obviously wrong."

"Yeah," Brad said. "Like his brain. His brain is wrong. He's losing it. There's no bear. There's just a—"

Brad stopped, staring off into the forest. I turned and saw the bushes shift, then I pointed toward the trees. DD lunged out of the forest, growling and snapping.

"Bear!" Brad screamed, his hands in the air, waving, like a commercial for screaming. Get your screams here! He turned and screamed louder, running for the lodge. We all took off after him and his screaming.

DD was actually totally scary. I actually wondered if I could really stop him. He looked like he was seriously ready to eat our eyes or something.

He roared, and Brad screamed even louder, waving his arms. Geez, Brad. SO loud. Maybe this wasn't the best idea. He was screaming nonstop, a bright, endless screech.

Seriously, he would be the first to go. If DD didn't eat his soul, the zombies were going to eat his brains...if he had any left. He worked out a lot. Like a lot.

"Stop screaming!" I told Brad. He had somehow dropped to the back of the pack. Maybe his stupid muscles were slowing him down. Everyone was sprinting ahead of him. I jogged along with him, looked back, and saw DD trotting along behind us, tailing wagging. He looked less like a demon and more like a dog. Okay. Things were looking up. Maybe no one would get eaten by zombies today. But then, glancing further back to the forest, I caught the eerie blue shine of the zombies. Uh-oh. Maybe not better. Maybe bad. Things were bad.

When I turned back, everyone else was almost inside.

"Go for the door, Brad! I'm cutting off toward the yardhouse! I'll distract the bear!"

"Good idea," Brad panted. He plodded on, without looking back.

It really wasn't a good idea. It was a stupid idea. But apparently Brad didn't care if a bear ate me. Seriously, I'm not really sure why he works at Camp Friendly Tree.

The zombies burst out of the forest as Brad slammed the front door closed.

Zombies!

It was just me and DD now. We cut around the lodge, heading for the tennis courts. I held my wings tight as I passed the yardhouse, waving my arms, convincing them to follow me. "Hey, Zombies! Come this way! Yum! Yum! I have brains! You want brains!"

They shot toward me, a flash of blue in the night. DD growled, but I urged him forward. "Come on! Not yet! Get to the fence!"

We ran for the fenced-in courts. The gate on the far side hung open. I'd need to get over there fast. But I had to get the front gate closed too.

Get them in the courts. Then call Nana. Or Dad. Or something. Plan. A great plan.

Zombies!

We ran into the tennis court, and they streamed after us. There were at least ten of them. DD seemed to understand the game, and he wasn't attacking them – he was just running around them in circles, bringing them closer to each other, like some sort of demon zombie cattledog. I jerked to the side, twisted around, and ran behind them. I locked the door we had just come in, then took off to the other side.

"DD!" I yelled. He barreled after me, rushed off the courts and out the gate, and I slammed the gate shut.

"Yes!" I yelled. I would have high-fived DD if he had hands. Instead, I petted his head as the zombies ran toward us. They were trapped.

Zombies!

Hopefully they weren't smart zombies that could open doors and stuff or do fractions. They didn't look like it, but what did smart zombies look like? And could they climb the fence? Or would they sprout wings? Call for dragons? Or would they just mill around? Were they dumb or super smart? And how would I know?

Zombies!

I stepped back and dug my feet in, forcing myself to watch. I needed to know what I was up against. At the last second, I opened my wings, just in case.

They slammed into the fence, clawing at the metal holding them back. They hit the bars, batted at the fence. It shook, but held solid.

I smiled. Time to call Nana. I reached into my pocket and pulled out her phone.

Wait – I had Nana's phone. How was I gonna call her? I'd have to call Dad. Tell him something to get him—

A zombie arm slashed at my face. I took a step back, scrolling through the phone and finding Dad's number. With the zombies stuck behind the fence...

My fingers stopped dialing. How was that zombie swinging its arm at me?

I looked up, and watched as its face slowly melted through the fence – like some blue Jell-O monster mold – and its face joined me on the other side. It's shoulders slowly slipped through, and I turned to bolt, leaping into the sky, but it must have grabbed my wing, because I swung around and slammed into the fence.

When I looked up, silvery blue eyes looked back at me, and then the zombie opened its mouth wide, wide, and wider still. Its blue teeth, razor sharp.

Zombies!

I stared at the brochures Nana had dropped on the table. The kids were literally holding hands around a giant, smiling pine tree. They were wearing shorts and t-shirts and some kind of weird green vests. They all looked so gosh darn happy about it.

"No," I said.

"Gwyn--" she started.

I didn't let her finish. "Nuh-uh. No way. I don't want to go there. Not even a little bitty bit. Nope."

"Of course you don't want to go there," Nana said. "Nobody wants to go there. That's the whole thing. It's a summer camp. Their family makes them go there."

I rolled my ocean rock along the table. "Why can't I just stay at home this summer like I usually do? Play basketball? Ride bikes? Go swimming?"

Nana wiped her hands on her pants, then sat down at the table beside me. "You need something more."

"Jaiden gets to stay home."

"His sister is there."

"I could go over there?"

"Not every day. She's not your babysitter."

"I'll stay home then."

"You need to get out."

"I want to stay here. With Dad. I want to be with you."

"I'll be working. And your dad has his research. And..." She watched my fingers tracing the table, then tapped her fingers along the same line. "It wouldn't be good. With your dad. Not right now. He needs some time to get back to himself."

"He doesn't need any more time to himself. He has tons of time to himself. He needs..." I sighed. I had no idea what he needed.

And honestly, I didn't care. It was always about him. Every day since she died. People were so worried about him.

"I don't want to go," I repeated.

"It won't be that bad," Nana said.

I sighed. "Have you even seen their stupid matching green vests?"

22

IT WAS BAD. THE ZOMBIE SNAPPED HIS BROKEN JAW, BLUE FLESH hanging down, reaching for my neck.

Zombies!

Was this real? How was this real? I kicked at the zombie, but my foot mushed into it, like applesauce. Ewww. I quickly pulled my leg back out. Gross. Weird. Dang. Yuck. Eww.

How do you fight something that isn't really there?

It grabbed my shirt and pulled me in toward its rotten blue face. I couldn't touch it, but it could touch me? Come on! Unfair!

I watched another zombie melt through the fence. It left a piece of cheek behind. Gross.

You don't fight that. You can't. You run.

I tore my shirt away just as DD dove at the zombie. He grabbed its arm and ripped it away with his wicked teeth. How was he doing that? He could get the zombie, but it was all applesauce to me.

Doesn't matter. Just run.

I sprinted full out, headed for the parking lot, where I could launch straight into the sky and get out of there. I glanced back at the lodge. I didn't want them to eat—

I stumbled over the curb and almost ran into the dark green car. It was parked in the fire lane. The shiny sportscar. And Brad. Still screaming.

"What?" I yelled, running toward the car. "What are you doing? You're supposed to be inside!"

He was fumbling with his keys. He screeched louder when he saw me, then shook his head and fumbled again at the lock. "Nope. I saw them. Out the window." He spat words at me, and pointed at the car. "In," he said, and opened the door. "Or don't. Whatever. I'm gone."

He jumped in, and I did too. I barely had enough time to close the door before he squealed out of the parking lot.

I wasn't thinking. It's a little problem I have. I get stressed out and make weird choices. But come on, there were zombies! Blue ones! Dripping blood and guts!

Still, I shouldn't have gotten in his car. I should have used my wings.

No. I was being brave, right? If Brad had zombies chasing him, he might need my help. And maybe I didn't want him to die. That last part was questionable. Still, Brad would helpful — a good distraction. They could chew on his head a little bit.

I turned and looked out the rear window. The zombies were hot on our tails. Or cold on our tails. Or blue. They were blue. And dead. And fast.

Zombies!

DD was running hard behind them, nipping at their heels and herding them toward us. Ugh. Demon zombie cattledog. That made me the zombie shepherd.

"Stupid Camp Friendly Tree," Brad said. "Every freaking year – it's something. First, the fire. Then, Sarah. And now, it's Night of the Living Dead. No freaking way. Dad can't make me work here. I'm going to Timberline this summer. Hanging out with..."

His words faded as I turned back around. He looked at me like he'd never seen me before. "When'd you get here? Who let you in?"

"You did," I said, in a moment of courage that is unlikely to ever repeat itself.

"I did not. This is my car. Get out."

He didn't slow down.

"No?" I said slowly. "There's zombies out there."

"What zombies?"

"The blue ones?"

"Ha! Smurf zombies. That would be hilarious. And creepy. You making a movie?"

"No," I said, searching for that glimmer of blue as we rounded a turn. "They are following us."

He looked at me like I had lost my mind.

Broken. That has to be it. Football ate his brain. Or drugs. He was like a big old pile of empty. Steroids. Did they do that? Make your brain dumb?

He sped up even faster, taking the sharp curves with a squeal. "Whatever. This is a 1983 Pontiac Trans Am. Fastest car in Portland. Maybe even Oregon. You're lucky to be in here. I usually don't drive kids around." He laughed like I was one of his buddies. "And you're a kid." Okay, I wasn't one of his buddies. "Seriously," he said. "Get out."

I looked back at the road and saw the glimmer of blue on the horizon. They were still following us. Hopefully DD was too. I wouldn't know until I got back up in the air.

"Okay," I said. "Let me out here."

"Do you have 20 bucks?" he asked.

I didn't.

"Yes."

"Cool," Brad said. "I'll give you a ride. I need gas. Where to?"

"Flicker. It's down by OMSI," I said.

"You're such a nerd."

"Yep," I said. No use arguing that.

"Your friend is cool though. He's so fast. Ridiculous on the court. It's mind-bending. Up in the air for hours. I've seen you miss a billion three-pointers, loser. What's your friend's name?"

"Jaiden." Brad should have known his name. After all, Brad was our counselor last year at Camp Friendly Tree. He was terrible. The worst. Jules was the only thing that made it bearable the first year, and it was finally okay when Jaiden joined us the next year.

But that was also the year we got Brad as a counselor, and a lot of noogies, wedgies, and loogies. Geez.

He turned and looked at me. "Why are you here?"

I smirked. "I gave you 20 bucks for gas. You're driving me down to the waterfront."

"Cool," Brad said. He reached into the backseat. "Want a protein bar?"

Ugh. Protein bars are like flavored chalk. But I needed food. Or at least calories. "Yes. I'm starving."

He passed me a bar, and I tore it open and took a bite. Some kind of grass powder bar. With chunks? I nearly gagged, but forced it down.

Brad swallowed his almost whole. "You could use more protein," he said. He was still chewing. "It would help you bulk up."

"I don't need to bulk up."

Brad looked at me like I was a screaming toddler. "Yeah you do. How are you going to make the varsity team?"

"What varsity team?"

"Ha!" Brad said. "You're funny. Not like your little friend. She gets so mad at me. All the time. It's weird."

"Jules?" I asked. She hated Brad with the intensity of a thousand suns. Seriously, she almost threw him in the bonfire last year.

"Who?" Brad asked.

"Nothing," I said.

"Why are you here?"

I sighed. "You're giving me a ride. I gave you 30 bucks."

"Awesome!" Brad said. He stared blankly at the road, then looked over at me. His jaw dropped, and he swerved, then readjusted. His large bicep shout out and he pointed over at me. "Why do you have wings?"

Zombies!

23

"Look out!" I yelled.

Brad slammed on the brakes, then swerved and screeched to a stop right before we hit Nana's car.

She was standing in front of her station wagon with her hands on her hips.

"What?!" I yelled.

Brad revved his engine. I glared at him. "What's she doing in the road?" he asked. Who is that?"

I unbuckled my seatbelt. "That's my nana. You know her. You met her last year."

"No, I didn't."

"Yes, you did. She yelled at you."

"No, she didn't."

"Well," I said. "She's probably going to."

I jumped out the car, then turned back to Brad. "Wait here," I said.

He put the car in reverse.

"Come on!" I said. "Just wait a minute!"

He turned the music on. "Hurry up," he said.

I held the door open, so he couldn't leave. "What are you doing?" I yelled to Nana.

"I need you to take these kids."

They were huddled in the backseat of the car. She opened the car door. "I have something I need to do."

Jules tumbled out of the car. "Gwyn!" she said, running over to me.

Jaiden jumped out behind her. "That was awesome! Straight up LOCA!"

"What happened?" I asked.

"We'll tell you in the car," Jules said.

Jaiden opened Brad's door to get in.

"Nope," Brad said. "Not gonna happen. Reserved seats. Not enough room."

"Brad!" Jules snapped. "You have a backseat!"

"That's not what it's for."

"Gross," I said. I pulled on the seat handle. "Besides," I said slowly. "I gave you 50 bucks."

"Sweet," he said. "But this is it. No more rides. I got stuff to do tonight."

"I'm sure you do," I said.

Jaiden climbed in. "I can't believe we're riding with Brad," he said.

"You're not," Brad said.

"Okay," Jaiden said. "Your car is amazing."

"Yeah it is!" Brad said, tapping the steering wheel. "Why are you in it?"

Jules hugged me, soft and quick. "I'm glad you're okay." I patted her back, this warm feeling hitting me. I didn't realize how cold it was until she put her hand on my shoulder. We both pulled away.

I glanced over at Nana. Her eyes narrowed in on Brad.

"What about Kai?" I asked. He was still in her car.

"He's got an idea. He's coming with me."

"Good!" Brad yelled.

"Shut-up," I said.

"See you at Flicker," Nana said.

"Okay!" I yelled back.

I squeezed into the car, squishing my wings into place.

"Dude," Brad said. "What's with the weird costume?"

"Shut-up, Brad," I said.

He puffed out his chest. "You want to go? I could take you. You're scrappy, but you're small. I could lift you with my pinky finger."

"I'm sure you could."

"Thanks."

"You're welcome."

"Why are you here?"

"Here we go again."

"What?"

"Why's he doing that?" Jules asked.

"He can't remember anything," I said.

"Yeah, I can! I got like a...number...on my ACT. I'm going to University of Oregon. Now, why are you here?"

"You're driving us to Flicker downtown. We're excited! We paid you 100 bucks."

"Wow. Awesome. Let's do this." He gunned the engine, I threw on my seatbelt, and we headed south for Portland on the weirdest road trip I've ever taken.

"Why's Brad even here?" Jules asked as we sped away.

"It's my car," he said. "You like it, right? It's a 1983 Pontiac Trans Am. Fastest car in Portland."

"He gave me a ride," I said.

Jaiden pushed my shoulder. "You don't need a ride. You have wings. You can FLY."

"I know. But I was a little stressed out, okay?"

"You guys are weird," Brad said. "All this nerd stuff. Dragons and whatever."

"And your Nana is loca!" Jaiden added. "She brought us to some creepy gas station."

"And there was a giant beaver," Jules said.

"Beaver?" Jaiden asked. "What are you talking about? It looked like a huge crocodile."

"Whatever it was," Jules said, "she was *talking* to it and it was talking back. So weird."

I shook my head in confusion. "Wait till you find out what happened at Camp Friendly Tree."

"Where friends are made," Jules said.

"That eat your brains!" I replied.

Brad ran straight through a red light. "You guys playing one of those nerd games? Duncan's and Dragons?"

"Yes," Jules said, very solemnly. "But there is no Dunkin Donuts involved. The beaver-crocodile ate them all in the crypts under Krispy Kreme Cathedral."

"I love donuts," Brad said.

"This is hilarious," Jaiden said.

"Shut-up, dweeb. What are you doing here anyway?"

"What are you writing?"
I snapped my book shut
and looked up. It was the
girl with all the red hair.
She wasn't looking at
at me, but she was
clearly talking to me.
"Nothing," I said.
"Can I sit by
you?" she mumbled.
"Sure." I said.
I moved my bag
so she could set
her stuff down on
the picnic table.
"Mom said I
have to make
more friends."
She opened up her
brown lunch bag. "That's why I'm here,
at Camp Friendly Tree, wasting my
summer. To make more friends."

"uh-huh," I mumbled, taking a huge PB&J bite.

"She said don't be shy."

I chewed hard, nodding.

"Because of the accident. Mom says it's just an arm." She set her arm on the table. I saw the shine of her prosthesis against the painted wood slats.

I swallowed a gigantic bite. "It is," I said.

"It is," she replied.

"I'm Gwyn," I said.

"Cool vest."

"Thanks. Yours looks dumb."

I laughed, and popped the collar. She laughed and popped hers too.

"Dumb vest," I said, straightening it back out. I knew we'd be friends.

24

"WE'RE ALMOST OUT OF GAS," BRAD SAID.

He'd forgotten about the zombies, and my wings too, but when I started to tell Jaiden and Jules about the zombies, he laughed super loud for like three minutes.

It was so awkward.

Jules couldn't sit still either. She had seen some supernatural-magic-confusing stuff with Nana, and didn't want to talk about it. Jaiden was taking it all in stride, loving this new world of beaver-crocodiles, wings, and Broken-Record-Brads. He hadn't met the zombies yet, though.

Zombies!

Before I knew it, we were turning toward the back of the Flicker parking lot.

"Jules," I said. "Jaiden. There's one other thing I need to explain."

"There is," Brad said. "I'm gonna run out of gas."

"I know," I said. "We talked about that." Four times. "There's a gas station around the corner."

"Where?" Brad said. "It's probably closed by now."

"My nana has a gas can," I lied. "In her car." I felt like a jerk, but seriously, we were in the middle of a zombie attack. I took off my seatbelt as he pulled into a parking space. "She's always worried about...running out of gas."

"That's really dangerous, you know," Brad said. "Her car could blow up. Someone could ram into her, and it would be like, BOOM!" His voice shook the car, and he got a crazy look in his eyes.

I scanned the parking lot, looking for Nana's car.

"Vroom!" Brad said, as headlights flashed toward us.

"Don't hit her car," I said.

"BOOM!" Brad yelled. He smiled, then looked over at me blankly. "What are you here for?"

"You're dropping us off."

"Us?" he asked, then jumped as he looked in the back of the car. "When did you all get here?"

Nana's car sped toward us.

"We're leaving," Jaiden said.

"Darn right you are!" Brad said. "Got any gas money?"

"Yes, just give me a second," Jules said, then shrugged.

"Wait a minute," Brad said. "Where are we?"

"Flicker. Where my dad works. His second job."

Brad stared at me blankly.

"It's a tech company," I said.

"You're going to a tech company in the middle of the night?"

"Yeah."

"Nerds."

"Yep," Jaiden said.

"Keep playing ball, kid," Brad said to Jaiden with a punch on the arm. "You're not terrible."

Jaiden beamed. "That is the most least mean thing you've ever said to me."

"Get out of my car," Brad said.

"Move it!" Nana yelled, slamming her car door.

"Coming!" I jumped out and let Jules and Jaiden out of the backseat.

"You okay?" Nana asked.

"Totally," I said. "Except—"

"What's that?" Jules asked.

I turned to see what she was looking at. The edge of the forest was shimmering blue.

"Zombies!" I said.

"Zombies?" Jules repeated.

"Zombies?" Jaiden asked, his voice a little too high. He stared at the far end of the parking lot toward a bank of warehouses. "How big are they? Can we take them? Do we have weapons? Are they going to eat our brains? We should hit them. In their heads. Aim for the cabeza, that's what I always say."

"Jaiden. You never say that," Jules said, watching the warehouses.

"Impossible," Kai said, walking over to us. "Zombies." He stopped in front of Brad's car, shaking his head.

Brad unrolled the passenger window. "What are you dudes talking about?"

"Gwyllion," Nana said.

"What?" I asked.

"They're not zombies," Nana said. "They're gwyll—"

"Bear!" Brad yelled. He turned the key to start his car, but it puttered, and promptly died. "Bear!" he screamed, then dove to the floor of the passenger seat.

DD bounded out from behind the bank of warehouses, and headed straight toward us. Brad looked up, screamed, and dove back into the passenger seat.

"It's okay!" I insisted. "The dog is with—"

"Dormarch!" Nana yelled, and he plowed into her, licking her hands and face. "What are you doing here?"

"That's not a bear," Jaiden mumbled, eyes wide. "That's a chupacabra. My hermano tells me stories. There's a lot of blood."

"Bear!" Brad yelled from deep in the car.

Jules sighed. "You all like to yell a lot."

DD backed away from Nana and sat down at my feet. "I've been calling him DD."

"What does DD stand for?" Jules asked reaching her hand out hesitantly. DD immediately covered it in dripping black demon dog drool.

"Demon Dog," I replied.

"That's not a dog," Jaiden whispered.

"Demon Dog," Nana said. "Makes sense. He works the Hell Mouth."

"Bueno," Jaiden said. "We have a chupacabra. That's great. Really." DD wagged his tail and Jaiden took a small step backwards. "But what's all this about zombies?"

"Gwyllion," Nana repeated.

"Zombies!" Brad screamed from inside the car.

"We need to go," Kai said. He was holding a large box in his two hands. It said LIVE on the outside.

"What's in the box?" I asked.

"Crickets," he said, holding it up. "For my snake. Well, they were for my snake. Now they are for our plan. We have a plan."

"There's snakes?" Brad yelled from inside the car.

"Zombies!" Jaiden yelled.

I turned to see what he was looking at, and found myself staring into a blue glow that was brighter than the sun.

"Whatever you do," Nana said, "do not let them touch you. We will break into two groups. Kai and I will head around the front and pull the zombies off your scent. You three take the side. Head to your Dad's office."

"Take DD," I said.

DD barked. His eyes were glued to the forest. Nana looked

that way, then shook her head. "No thanks. I have my birds. And you're going to need him." She patted him on the head. He nuzzled into her hand, all teeth and drool and demon.

"Bear!" Brad screamed.

"What about Brad?" I asked.

"I don't want him," Nana said. "He's got a tynged – a glamour – a spell. It's crawling all over him. He's useless. I wonder what he did. I want not part of that. You take him."

"A tynged?" I asked. "No way. You told me about those spells. They are the worst."

"Exactly," Nana said. "He's your friend. You take him."

"He's not my friend!" I snapped.

"Dude," Brad said. "Uncool." He looked over at DD and started screaming again.

"Does he stop?" Nana asked.

"In about a minute," Jules replied.

"Nana," I said. "He clearly needs your help."

"Nah," Nana said. "Let them eat him."

"Nana!"

"What? We've lost many souls to gwyllion. He won't be the first to fall." I opened my mouth to complain, but she sighed dramatically. "If you're going to get all particular about it, you keep him. Just get him out of the way."

"How?" I asked, throwing my hands in the air. "I couldn't even get him out the car."

"We don't have time for this," Kai said.

Jules leaned through Brad's window. "Let's go, loser."

"But—"

"Now!" she yelled.

He scrambled up. "You don't need to get so mad." He grabbed his keys from the ignition, opened the door, and slammed it shut. He locked the door – even though the window was still open – and turned back toward her. "Seriously. It's not like—" He caught sight of DD again. "Bear!" he yelled, then ran off toward the entrance.

"Ha!" I yelled to Nana. "He's yours!" She sighed, but took off after him. I could hear her yelling as we headed toward the side doors.

I burst into the kitchen, dripping
mud and dirty water.

Mom was coughing, but she threw
her hands in the air when I ran
through the door. "Don't come racing
in here like you have the wild hunt on
your heels. Take off those shoes and
tell me what happened."

Her eyes were puffy, but I didn't
ask. I pulled off my muddy shoes, socks

Splorching, dripping and sticking as I ripped them out of my shoes. "Sorry. Ewwwww. Creek. Gross. Jaiden made me--"

She whipped out a towel. "Ain't nobody made you do anything," she said with a snap of her towel. "Unless you got a tynged, and you're smart enough to get out of that one, or not get into one in the first place."

"What's a tynged anyway?" I asked.

She tossed the towel in my face. "It's a compulsion, a spell. Someone makes you do or not do something. The most famous one is in the Mabinogian--"

"Where all your favorite Welsh myths and stories are," I said.

"Not even. You haven't heard the half of them. But the Mabinogian makes it easy, telling all those tales in ways we can understand."

"Like Arianrhod?"

Mom's head shot up, eyes widening. She looked like she had seen a ghost, or I knew something I shouldn't. "What was that, honey?" she asked.

"Arianrhod. Didn't she do that spell thing to her kid? Super weird."

Mom's face relaxed. "Yes! Now that's a constellation worth knowing. Forget Arthur's Chariot. Caer Arianrhod shines. They say when all the sparks ignite, and the Northern Crown aligns, Arianthod will finally open her door. When the Goddess of the Silver Wheel takes flight, darkness will become light." Her face was shining, like she was sending me a message through the centuries over that muddy creek and straight into our kitchen.

When she got like that, I had no idea what to say, except to look at her, and listen, and hope with every bit of me that some little piece of what she said was true.

Darkness will become light

25

I WANTED TO FLY – MY WINGS WERE ITCHING TO TAKE OFF – BUT I didn't want to leave my friends behind. I pulled my mantle down to free my wings. I know my clothes weren't real, but they felt real. And I needed to be thinking clearly.

Just then Nana's owls swooped down, flooding the sky. Brad was going to love that. He was going to straight up lose it. But then he'd probably forget it, too.

DD cut ahead of us, and we ran even faster.

"Zombies?" Jaiden asked.

"I know," I panted.

"This is awesome," he said. "It's like a horror movie!"

"I would really like to survive," I said, already panting. Jules was kicking it beside me. "You good?" I asked.

"Yep," she said. "I'm still the fastest runner." She sprinted to the door, and Jaiden rushed after her. They pulled on the doors, but they were locked, and the lights were low. I ran up and pounded on the door. If Mike – the security guard – was in there, he'd open the door for me.

We pounded again and waited a moment, but he didn't come. Maybe he had fallen asleep again?

"Time's up," I said. "DD?" He bounded up beside me. I backed away and pointed at the door. Jules and Jaiden scrambled out of the way as DD dug his claws into the cement, barreled toward the door and, without any hesitation, crashed through the glass.

"Asombroso," Jaiden said.

"Totally," Jules added. "He's better than K-9."

"Who?" Jaiden asked, following DD through the broken doorway.

Jules sighed. "Kazan?" Jaiden shook his head. "Cujo?" He shook his head again. "Fine. He's a really cool dog."

"He's a chupacabra!" Jaiden said. DD shook off the shards of glass and trotted back toward us. Jaiden swerved around DD and the broken glass and headed for the stairs. "Vámonos!"

I scratched DD's ear, and he nudged into me. We took off after Jaiden. It seemed like it was going to be easy, but then a light flashed in the corridor, and we all froze.

Someone stomped toward us, and DD raised his hackles. "Easy boy," I said as Mike rounded the corner. I pulled my wings in tight.

"You can't be—" He stopped, staring first at the glass, then at the dog, then at us. He took a step toward me, and DD growled low.

"It's okay," I said to DD, and patted his flank. Mike's eyes widened, and his hand settled on his nightstick. "I'm sorry, Mike. It's an emergency. We had to break in. We have to see my dad right now."

His hand shook as he ran it over his bald head. "Okay, Gwyn. Okay. Okay. But we can't have animals in here. Or whatever that thing is. I'm going to have to—"

"Call the police," I finished. "Right now. Yes! You do that. We're going upstairs."

"Okay," he repeated.

"Okay," I said.

He turned and headed back toward the office, but then he stopped. "Gwyn. I'm...I'm glad you're safe. I was worried about you. Earlier. You were on the news."

"Thanks, Mike." He turned to go, and I ran my hand through my hair. "Hey, Mike. Um...you might want to hide. In your office. Lock the door. There's some weird stuff going on."

Mike turned back, looked at DD, then nodded his head. "Yes. Weird stuff. This place. Terrible. I need a new job." He spun around and hurried back toward the office. I'd never seen him move so fast in my life.

We ran to the stairs, the sounds of crashing windows over by the front entrance. Nana and Kai were on their way in too, along with Brad, her owls, and an incoming horde of zombies. They were going to scare the stuffing out of Mike.

As we ran up the stairs, I had a flash of déjà vu – running up the stairs again, just like this morning at OMSI. Only this time, instead of being chased by a giant ball of light, that light was now inside me, and zombies were chasing me instead.

Ridiculous. I was wiped out. That's the best way to describe it. My feet slogged, and my brain slogged too. The day was unending – just like science class with Dad. He'd drone on endlessly, and get excited about the weirdest stuff. Things that didn't even matter, like vacuums. Who cares about vacuums? Dad does. A lot. He had us make 23 tiny vacuums at the start of the year. We didn't even do anything with them – just talked about which design was most effective and why. He liked my motor, but thought my suction was "a little uneven."

"Would you say it sucked?" I asked.

He didn't think that was very funny. Jaiden did though. I heard him laugh.

Man, what I wouldn't give to have skipped the field trip to OMSI altogether. To just have had another boring day in Dad's class making vacuums. To never have walked into the giant glass monstrosity and all the zombies.

But then, I wouldn't have wings.

"What's with the zombies?" Jules asked as we passed the second floor. "Were they trying to eat you?"

"I don't know. They were really weird. They wouldn't stop chasing me. And you can't touch them. But DD can. Oh, and they're blue. They glow."

Jules laughed, and it echoed up the stairwell. "Like giant zombie smurfs?"

"Exactly," I said.

"Loco," Jaiden said. "This whole thing. But also awesome. Those wings are awesome. The zombies though. And the beaver—"

"Crocodile," Jules interrupted.

"That was loco," Jaiden finished.

"You know," Jules added. "Your Nana told us to just believe all the stories are true. That anything is possible."

"She told me that too."

"But I have no idea what to expect," Jules continued. "I've never heard this story before."

"Me neither," I said. "I'm hoping for a happy ending."

We stopped at the third floor, staring up at the door marked STAFF ONLY.

Jules slowly and methodically pulled her sleeve up, tucking it over the top of her prosthesis. "Well, it doesn't matter. I think we make our own happy endings, anyway. So let's get to work."

I nodded my head, and braced myself. "DD!" I yelled, and Jaiden and I stepped out of the way as he bounded up the rest of the stairs.

"Wait!" Jules yelled. DD skittered to a stop as Jules reached out and turned the door knob. The door opened right up. She held it for me, her eyebrows raised as we walked through. "We don't need to break everything, Wylde."

"Dude. He is gonna kill you," Jaiden said.

I swallowed hard. "No. He's not. He's at the doctor's office. With Mom. Again. It'll be fine." I repeated the words to myself in my head. It'll be fine.

"Let's clean it up," Jules said.

"It's a window," Jaiden said. "It's still gonna be super obvious when he gets back. There's a giant hole. With air coming through it and stuff."

My stomach flipped, but I kept my cool. "I got this. You guys should go."

Jules picked up the ball. "Nah. We're in this together."

Jaiden shook his head. "He's gonna kill all of us. Permanentemente."

"Yep," Jules said, and I sighed.

Jaiden shrugged. "Bien. We got this. Where's the broom?"

26

I smiled, and headed into the office. Jules was right – we didn't need to break everything.

Someone didn't get that message, though. The office was destroyed – chairs overturned and papers scattered, all leading toward the lab in the back.

"Somebody's been through here," Jules said.

"And they made a mess," Jaiden added, kicking a broken cardboard box out of the way.

"Shh," Jules whispered.

"Okay," Jaiden whispered back, and we both laughed. Jules rolled her eyes.

We looked down the dark hallway toward the lab. "You know what's back there?" Jules asked.

"Nope. Dad never lets me into the lab. Because: reasons."

"Because: lair," Jaiden said.

"Because: liar," I added. I pushed my glasses up again. I must have busted them when I dropped them at OMSI.

"Should we go in?" Jules asked, squinting down the narrow hallway.

"Let's wait a second for Nana," I said.

Jules picked up a paper, then let it fall. "They must keep them back there. The sparks."

She clicked her tongue, and I looked over at her. "What?" I asked. "What are you thinking?"

"Do you think...um...well, do you think your dad really is, like, a bad guy?"

I kicked the paper at my feet. "I don't think he could ever be a really bad guy. Not like the movies or anything. But, I think he could do bad stuff, you know? Like, accidentally? He's so laser-focused on what he's doing, I think he could miss the big picture, and make some really bad choices for good reasons."

Jules sighed. "I think that's most of us."

"Yeah," I said. "But the thing is, my dad, he doesn't see the good anymore. He doesn't have anyone to stop him, or show him what's right. He doesn't care."

"I don't think that's true," Jules said. "He cares about you. And he has you."

"Totally," Jaiden said, snapping me with his rubber band. I tried to snatch it from him, but he wrapped it back up in his hair again. "He cares a lot. He just totally sucks at it. He always has. He's the worst."

I didn't argue that. Jaiden was right. Dad really is not good at being a dad anymore. Or a person. I mean, it just didn't make sense to me that he had all those sparks. Did he know? Did he even understand what they were? Where they came from?

Jules nudged my arm. "You should let your wings loose. You might need them."

"It's okay," I said. "They're loose. This shirt...it's not real."

"Sure," Jaiden said. "Whatever."

But Jules smiled. "Cool."

I caught a whiff of something. It smelled like burning. "Guys, do you smell smoke?"

They both sniffed hard. "I do," Jules said.

Jaiden rubbed his hands on his pants. "We should stop

waiting. We need to get in there."

DD whined, and I jumped. He was so quiet behind me, I kind of forgot he was there. I patted his head, and then nodded my own. "Okay. Let's go. We've waited long enough. We need to free those sparks before the zombies eat us."

Jaiden laughed, and Jules shushed him. "Oh, come on," he said. "That sounded super dumb."

"Wait until you see them up close," I said.

"I'll punch them in the face," Jaiden said.

"They're like applesauce," I said, remembering how my hand had squished into one of the zombies.

"Eww," Jules said.

"Awesome," Jaiden said. "Like punching a bowl of Jell-O."

Jules gagged. "That is so not awesome."

We tiptoed down the hall toward Dad's lab. At least we had a giant demon dog. I mean, we'd still have to figure how to hack our way through the security or the keypad or—

The door was open. Just a crack, but it hadn't slid all the way shut. A low beep was coming from the keypad, along with a stream of smoke. The burning filled my nose and mouth. What happened?

I looked at Jules, and she reached out to slide the door open the rest of the way. "Ready?" she whispered.

"Wait," Jaiden whispered. "The dog first. He'll eat their brains." DD nudged Jaiden's leg, and Jaiden squeaked.

We stopped. Breath held. Did they hear us?

I punched Jaiden in the arm, and DD nudged him again. He gritted his teeth. "Tell the dog to stop touching me and go eat their souls."

Jules ignored him. "Don't make DD go first," she whispered. "Get him behind us. They won't know he's here."

I smiled at Jules, and she nodded back. That sounded like a plan. An actual plan. As for the rest, well, we'd find out when we pushed open the door.

WORK
WORK
WOR
WO
W

"Gwyn, you have to let him work."

I looked over at her face, and that clear strip of skin above her nose. Not her eyes. They were bright red. Bloodshot. Not hers. Not my mom's.

"Come on," I mumbled, fingers rubbing her thin cotton sheet. "He works every day. All the time."

"He needs it," she sighed. Her breath rattled in her chest.

I focused on the sound of her heart monitor, the beeps and dips that covered the coughs and the breaths and all the aching. The sounds of life.

"It's not going to be easy. He won't have anything once I'm gone."

"Stop talking like that. You'll be fine." I still couldn't meet her eyes. Anything but her eyes. "Besides, he'll be okay. he's got me."

She touched my cheek, turned her chin toward mine. "I know. And you'll have him. But it will take him time. Time to find his way back. He's already so far gone. You'll have to be strong. Deep inside. You'll have to remember who you are. Who he was. And most of all, you'll have to be more than most of us. You'll have to shine.

27

THE DOOR WAS HEAVY, STUCK ON ITS TRACKS. JULES SHOVED IT hard, and it squeaked out of the way. I slipped through first, eyes scanning the lab.

"Dad!" I yelled.

He was pressed up against a shining metal table, gasping for air. Unbelievably, Wythe had his hand on my Dad's throat.

"Good," he said. "You're here. I was just telling your father not to free the sparks. I'm sure you'll make a compelling argument before I break his neck."

I stole a glance behind Dad where a large pane of glass lit up the room. Sparks swirled through the air behind it, dancing through the air like a tornado of light. They were beautiful – shifting and flashing behind the glass. My chest ached to see them trapped, and a fire lit within me. I took a step closer to the window. We needed to get them out of there. But Dad—

"Let him go," I said.

"No," Wythe said. "That's not how this works. Don't be a child. We need those sparks. We're not just letting them go."

Jules stepped up beside me, and Jaiden appeared on my left.

Dad mumbled something, and Wythe opened his mouth, but I refused to listen to his big villain speech. We'd waited long enough. I nodded at Jaiden, and he stepped out of the way.

DD barreled past us. His claws tore through the tile as he bounded for Wythe. Instantly, Wythe spun away, throwing Dad at DD, but the dog clomped to the side and jumped for Wythe.

Metal crashed behind us, and I spun around to see a rotting arm, pale blue and shining, reach slowly through the doorway, like a bad horror movie.

"Run!" I yelled.

Jules and Jaiden cut around to the side of the lab. I bolted after them.

Wythe cried out and struggled with DD on the ground. Dad was on his hands and knees, holding his throat. He reached out and pointed toward a control panel. I grabbed his arm, hauled him up, and pulled him toward the panel.

"Grab that trashcan!" Jules yelled.

I glanced back at Jules – she swung an umbrella through the air, then pointed it forward, and drove it into the zombie. The umbrella cut right through it. She swung her prosthetic arm hard at the zombie as she fell forward, and the metal blazed red and cut in deep. The zombie screeched, long and loud. She pushed it back! Her prosthesis blazed red and some- how, she could touch the bright blue zombies. They cringed away from her.

"It's the metal." Dad's voice came out raw.

Julia stared down at her hand. The color faded, and she pulled herself up to her feet, and held out her umbrella in one hand and her arm out in front of her. Two more zombies pushed their way into the room. I shoved Dad toward the control panels and grabbed the rolling chair, then kicked it hard into a zombie. It stumbled, but didn't stop, until Jules whacked it in the face with a fiery flash, sending it flying across the room.

"What is happening?" she yelled.

"It's the metal!" I yelled back. Jaiden launched a book, a lamp, and then a computer at the mass of zombies writhing their way through the door. It distracted them, but didn't stop them. "Hurry up!" I yelled back at Dad. The zombies kept coming – so many that they bottlenecked at the door. We tried to keep them there.

I glanced back at the control panel. Dad was just staring at the screen. "What are you waiting for?" I yelled.

"It's updating," he choked out. "Stupid program. I just need to get to the desktop. I can open the door right from—"

Wythe slammed into Dad, knocking him from the console. Dad crashed to the ground. DD sprung after Wythe again. I reached down, but something fell into me, and I stumbled to the side. I kicked the zombie off me, but my foot only smacked its face for a second, and then pushed right through. The zombie smiled, its bleu teeth dangling.

"DD!" I yelled, but he was clawing at Wythe and tearing a zombie off of Jules. She threw her umbrella and tripped the next one that came through the door, slicing its blue rotting flesh.

Zombies!

I scrambled away from the zombie, but then three more were there. Jaiden hit one in the head, but the others tumbled onto Jules and she fought them off, her arm slicing and blazing.

I ran to help, but Wythe grabbed my arm and pulled me tight. His face was inches from mine.

"Okay," he said. You've made your point. But this is ridiculous. Stupid. You kids have no idea what you are doing. I'll put an end to this." He ripped out a pair of handcuffs, and watched another zombie dive onto Jules. He stepped in front of me, his arm holding me back protectively. "Watch out! We need to get this under control. It's unsafe." He lifted the handcuff toward the zombie, but then spun around and slammed it onto my wrist.

"But—"

He jerked me forward and closed the other cuff around the leg of the console.

"There. That's better. I can work with the gwyllion—"

I wrenched my arm, but it held tight. "What are you talking about?" I spat back at him. "Wake up! They're going to eat your brains!"

"We'll need to study them. Are they matter? Some seem more solid. It's hard to tell."

"What are you talking about? They're zombies! Who cares? Get rid of them!" I ripped the cuff back and forth, trying to pull my arm loose. Dad was sprawled on the floor beside me. I wanted to scream. Wythe tricked me. I couldn't believe I thought he was going to help us. "You have to stop them. They're hurting Jules! They're hurting my friends!" The zombies had overwhelmed both Jules and Jaiden, and more were flowing through the door.

Suddenly, one launched into the air in a cloud of blue. When the fog cleared, Kai stood at the door, his arms full of office supplies. He threw opened a box of paper clips and launched them into the sky. The zombies ignited, flashing blue and black.

"Stop that!" Wythe yelled.

I kicked Dad with my foot. He didn't even budge — he was out cold. If Kai was here, though, Nana wasn't far behind. Help was on its way.

Wythe marched toward Kai, stepping over writhing zombies. "You are ruining everything!"

I looked back at the monitor. The desktop had finally loaded. I narrowed my eyes, staring hard at the screen.

Found it. A giant open door button. Super obvious. Thanks, Dad. This was going to be easy.

I raised my hand, reached up to the console, stretching as far as I could to tap the screen, but a zombie grabbed my wrist.

What to Expect

In the movies, when someone
is dead or dying, they're either a
flesh-eating zombie or lying on their
deathbed. If they're in a hospital bed,
they're pale and white and old.

Mom was different. She was 42.
Her hair wasn't grey. It was gone. Her
hair should have been black. Her skin
should have been deep brown.

But it was blue. And cold. Her lips
were chapped. She grunted with every
single breath. She groaned and cried
and barely closed her eyes.

They gave me a pamphlet called
**What to expect when a person
with cancer is nearing death.**
What stuck in my head, what made
me shake beside her hospital bed,
what made my throat close and click,
made me lose sleep and stare

blankly at the walls, it wasn't the words in the pamphlet, or that she was gasping for every breath. What scared me most is that they knew it was coming.

Someone, at some point, had time to make a **pamphlet**. They had time to fix the fonts and double check the spelling. They even drew a cartoon. They planned it all out, and they knew that now was the time I should read it. It was like they were checking boxes off a list:

28

I SHOVED THAT ZOMBIE OFF ME, BUT MY HANDS SUNK INTO THE applesauce, and somehow it held tight, tighter, until it wasn't, it couldn't – it pushed right into me.

I screamed, and its hand disappeared into mine.

How did it – I tried, I pulled, I yanked. I could feel it inside me, pushing against my skin. It didn't just go through me – the zombie's arm was somehow melting into mine. It was in me. How did I stop it? I couldn't—

DD lunged at the zombie, knocking it to the ground. I fell with him, my wrist tearing against the handcuff. DD wrestled the zombie, dragging my arm back and forth until suddenly – the zombie's arm ripped off and they both crashed into a shelf.

I stared down at my arm. No. Not my arm. It was shot through with blue. Glowing. Dark. Twisting. The zombie's hand was still inside me.

DD tossed the zombie into the air, then ran back for Jaiden, who was fighting off two nearly invisible zombies with the umbrella. Jules had lifted a computer, and was literally throwing it at Wylde. She was amazing.

I pushed through the pain. This had to be the end. I reached up my cracking, bending fingers, then pounded my hand hard against the button.

The door burst open in a flood of light, and Kai threw his crickets into the air.

The Real Ending

"When the darkness came, and took their wings, they sent one small spark of light across the ocean. They hoped, they dreamed, that one day, the **spark** would return to them when they called."

She leaned back against the hospital bed, the story finished. Reality returned and the monitor beeped again. I wished I could fall back into her story and not come back up.

"What is it, Mom?" I asked, rubbing her paper thin hand as she dragged in another breath.

"The spark?"

"Yeah."

"It's **magic**," she whispered, smiling faintly. "It's life. It's hope. It's all that delicious **possibility**."

"And what happened to the people? When they lost their sparks?"

"They fell into darkness. But they're waiting for the light. They're waiting for you."

29

She told me. So many times. I just didn't understand. But the truth flooded toward me in that blaze of light.

The sparks filled me with hope.

Then, they crashed into zombies. Collided with the crickets. Burned through Wythe. One hit Jules as she pulled Jaiden to his feet, and two slammed into a zombie, and then collided with Kai. They all crashed to the ground. The rest o the sparks flew out the door, disappeared through the walls, and headed out into the world.

The air sizzled, a zombie screamed, and then the lab was quiet. Too quiet.

Wythe had blown back toward me. He was out cold. I dragged him closer, searched his pockets for the handcuff key, and set to work on my cuffs. Dad was stirring, mumbling quietly about anti-matter. I don't know if he was dreaming or awake. My cuff clicked open, and I grabbed the zombie closest to me. My hand slipped through, so I reached out with my other hand – my blue hand – and I grabbed it tight. My hand pulsed as I dragged the zombie up and pulled it into the glass enclosure.

The gwyllion were applesauce in my regular hand, but I could pick them up with my zombie hand.

"Jules!" I yelled. "Jaiden! Are you okay?"

Jules was on her knees, coughing, hacking, but she was breathing, and that was enough.

"I'm good," Jaiden yelled back. "I've got Kai."

I didn't even think. I just got to work. If I could get the zombies in that big glass room before they woke back up, I could close the door and make them spin like those sparks did. Boom. No more zombies.

Jules saw what I was doing and stumbled toward me. She tried to grab a zombie, but her hand went right through it.

Crack! Her body popped and she fell into me. "Jules!" I pulled her in close. I held her tight as she trembled and jerked. Her chest filled with light, and then wings burst from her back.

They were beautiful. Tan and white and etched with gold. How was it possible? Dazzling. Blinding. I stared at her, mouth open, hands holding so much wonder. How could the world be full of so much light?

Pop! Crack. Screech.

The room filled with sound.

Uh-oh.

The zombies. They writhed on the ground, light pulsing through them, surrounded by tiny crickets that were crawling across the floor. I watched as a zombie screeched and stretched, then pop! Leathery, black wings shot out of its back. Wythe and Kai trembled on the floor, while wings popped out of the crickets too.

"Seriously?" Jaiden said.

"Come on!" I said. "Grab the crickets!" They were already bursting into the air, tiny black wings beating. "I'll get the rest of the zombies!"

They were waking up, wings stretching toward the ceiling. I

set Julia down gently and grabbed another zombie, dragging it into the enclosure. DD dropped the last one at my feet, and I heaved it in and ran out of the enclosure.

Wythe writhed on the floor, moaning. Could we put him in there? Would the spinning scramble his brain? We had to stop him. Maybe we could cuff him? Where were the cuffs? What would hold him? There's no telling what he—

Kai cried out and rolled over. With a grinding pop – like metal on metal – scaly, massive wings shot out of his back. Huge, blue, and shining.

His dad crawled toward him, and Jaiden ran over. He grabbed Wythe's arm, but before he could restrain him, his body flashed with light and his wings cracked out, smashing into Jaiden, who flew across the room and straight into the enclosure.

Wythe stood up, his body lengthening, his long, leather wings stretching wide. He picked up a table and smashed it into me. I fell to the ground, hands breaking my fall, but cracked my head against the tile. A shock of pain and dark settled in, but I shook it off, bits of light trickling into my eyes. As my vision cleared, Wythe grabbed my ankle and dragged me across the room. I kicked and screamed as he threw me into the enclosure.

I landed near a pile of blue applesauce. No. Not applesauce. A zombie! I caught Jaiden's eye and crawled for the door, pushing past the leg of a screaming zombie. A hand clamped down on my leg, and I kicked it hard, but it swung me backward and flipped me over, my wings crushed beneath me.

I looked up into the fiery eyes of Wythe.

"Gwyn. We all know where this is headed. Don't you understand? Didn't your Nana ever tell you? I've read the Mabinogion — studied it's secrets. The ancient Welsh stories have come back to life. I know who you are. I figured you out. And you can't return to the other side of the mountain. I need you here.

Locked up. Powerless. We'll turn on the rotating fields, close the glass enclosure – no one will ever know you're here. And the gwyllion can take care of your little friends."

"Stop it!" Jaiden yelled. Two zombies had grabbed his arms. He smacked them with his wings, but they had latched on tight. They were real, solid, and hungry.

"He'll be the first. You've seen the gwyllion feed – look down at your arm. It's not a pretty sight. When they decide to eat you, they turn from mist to flesh. They consume you. I saw one near the Humber. They're night wanderers. They won't eat his body – they'll feast on his soul."

"That's stupid," Jaiden said, punching one in the face. The gwyllion still clung to his arms.

"Walk to the back of the room," Wythe said. "Put your hands on the wall. I'll get your little friends in here—"

"No." Kai stood at the door, his wings indigo and shining, blocking out the light. "We're not staying."

My blue hand shook, my fingers lengthening then shortening. I crushed them into a fist.

Wythe nodded stiffly. "Of course you're not, Kai. We have work to do. Sparks to consume. You're ready now. You're coming with us."

Kai tilted his head. "If you had listened to me, if you had paid any attention, you would know that the Second Law of Thermodynamics states that the entropy of an isolated system always increases."

"I don't know what that has to do with anything—"

Kai slammed his hand against a desk. "Just listen, Dad! It means that if we think of this room as an isolated system, if we don't clean it up, take care of things, it will just keep getting more and more messy."

Wythe took a deep breath, and let it out slowly and carefully. Kai was dancing on the edge of a knife, and we were all going to get cut. "Do you have a point, son?" Wythe said, his voice like a growl.

"No," Kai said, and his face brightened. "I was just waiting for the owls."

Nana burst through the door, a flock of wings barreling behind her. I dove out of DD's way as he crashed toward Jaiden, ripping off his zombies, and I ran for the door, just as Nana slashed her way through the gwyllion.

Her eyes were a beam of golden light, and her smile was terrible. I grabbed Jaiden's arm as the owls swarmed around the screeching gwyllion, and we shoved our way out of the glass enclosure.

Kai collided with Wythe in a burst of light. Wythe grabbed his wing and shoved him toward the glass. A flurry of owls caught Kai and carried him toward us.

"You can't stop us," Wythe yelled. "We're stronger than you. Your time is over."

Nana laughed. "That's ridiculous. I'm older than rainbows, and you're just a piece of glass in a haystack. I don't need to fight you. I just need to close the door."

Wythe ran at her full speed. She twisted around and grabbed his wing, flipping him to the ground. He reached for her foot, but then she dissolved – disappeared – no! She turned into an owl!

I ran for the computer, found the button, and smashed my hand on it. The monitor fell backwards, and I grabbed a hold of it, tapping the close door button until it turned red.

The owls shot out of the enclosure. The door slammed shut. Feathers passed over me. The owls whirled through the air. I hoped one of them was Nana. I watched as they flew back out the window, but the last one stopped, shimmered, and unfolded beside the blinds.

Nana.

I ran to her, tripping over office supplies, feet flying through staples, tumbling toward her. I collapsed into her arms. She folded me in.

"It's okay," she mumbled into my hair, her hands pressed tight against my wings. Warm. Soft. Safe. I pushed my face in. "You're okay. You're okay."

I heard the sizzling of electricity, the whir of the fields, but I didn't raise my head. I couldn't. I breathed hard, counting in my breath, willing my pulse to slow.

Bang! My head shot toward the glass enclosure. Were they free? No! We had to stop them.

My eyes landed on the doorway. Wythe pounded on the glass, and a gwyllion arm snaked by the window. They were trapped and we were safe. For now.

"The fields are on," Kai said. "He can't hurt us. He's not going anywhere."

I clung to Nana, watching in horror as Wythe began to spin. The zombies pulled in toward him, and he pushed his wings against them, fighting off the swirling mass.

"We can't leave him in there," Kai said. "But let him work off some of his energy."

We all watched him spinning around, smacking zombies with his giant wings.

Jaiden made a barfing sound. "It's like the worst ride at Oaks Park. He's totally going to puke."

"So gross," Jules said.

Nana pulled back, her eyes settling into mine. They were brown again, with just a fleck of gold. "I'm so proud of you."

"You're an owl," I said, and she laughed, a great, big shaking laugh that pushed away the darkness.

"And so I am. You know what they say, Gwyn. Twirly bird gets the worm."

"Or the zombie," I said, which totally didn't make any sense, except it kind of did.

I took a breath, a deep one, and pushed the fear away like I was blowing out a candle. We could handle this.

A cricket flew by my nose, fluttering black, and Nana reached out and grabbed it. "Come on," she said. "We have so many crickets to catch!"

Nana held
my hand
outside the
church. The
rain poured
down, soaking
the ground and
running down
my face. Nana's
grip was hard, her
fingers all bone.
    I held tight too.
"She's gone," I
said. The words
felt impossibly big
in my mouth. They felt
horrible. Wrong.
    She sighed, that low
deep sigh I'd heard so many
times those last days. "Not really.
Not far. The worlds are closer than
you think. Life and love are powerful,

Gwyn.
She is
here
with you.
Always. And
she will be right
here whenever you
need her. No matter
what. She'll never leave
you. She loves you."
I wanted to say no, to
pull my hand away. Nana was
wrong. Mom was gone. She was
never, ever coming back.
They put her in the ground.
But at the same time, I held
my breath and felt the rain drip
down my cheek. I watched the
clouds gathering in that grey October
sky, then I took a breath that filled
me all the way to the top.
I wanted to believe.

30

WE SPENT THE NEXT FEW MINUTES CHASING DOWN CRICKETS. Their tiny bodies gleamed with a golden light. Wythe raged inside the enclosure, the zombies screeching around him, but we couldn't hear him. It was surreal.

Nana said he'd be fine, at least for a little while. The zombies couldn't feed inside the vacuum. She said she'd deal with Wythe later.

"The Afanc will help," she told us.

"The beavers?" Jules asked.

"The crocodiles," Jaiden shuddered.

"They are all things at once. Just like you."

Kai shook his head, his eyes landing on the glass enclosure. He didn't say anything, but I saw Nana whispering to him as she examined his wings. They were amazing. Like a dragon.

Later, we'd find out that the security cameras were all broken, that those other men in suits were unconscious, and that there had been a major gas leak. The Feds had the place blocked off for weeks.

But at that moment, we were worried about the fallout, and we needed a plan. We needed the work – to keep ourselves occupied while we figured out what came next. We cleaned up while Nana told us what we were going to do.

"The sparks must be returned," Nana said. "The doors reopened so the gwyllion can go home. You'll go to the other side of the mountain."

I stilled my broom. "What? Really? Where is it?"

Nana smiled. "You know how to get there.'"

I thought back for a moment, wondered if Mom had ever told me. But then I remembered. "The lines?" I asked, and she nodded.

"What lines?" Jules asked.

"I see them," I said. "On the ground. They tell me where to go."

"Instincts," Kai said.

"GPS," Jaiden added.

"Similar to a goose," Kai continued. "You are following a flight path."

Jaiden shook his head. "I can't believe you guys have wings." His shoulders sagged as he shoved papers into a pile on Dad's desk.

"Sorry, man," I mumbled. It sucked that Jaiden didn't get any. My hand jerked suddenly, a shocking spasm. I tucked it in my pocket, covering it up. My fingers stretched back out on their own, then pulled back in again. What was happening? My fingertips ached.

"You'll be fine," Nana said. I thought she was talking to me, but her eyes were on Jaiden. "I have something you can use."

Jaiden's eyes lit up, and he started grilling her, but Nana hushed him, refusing to tell him what it was.

"It better be chino," Jaiden said.

"It will be," Nana said with a smile. "It's kingly."

Jaiden started grilling her again.

The ceiling shifted above us, and Dad stepped away from the control panel. A wall emerged from the ceiling tiles, cut through the air, and touched down gently against the floor, sealing off the enclosure. I stared at the posters that were glued to the wall – it was like that room never existed. So cool. And so creepy. This was definitely a lair and not a lab.

Dad tapped the wall, then turned back toward us. "We still have to deal with them."

"We do," Nana said. "But he's not strong enough yet. And if he wants to hunt, he will need the bow."

I opened my mouth to ask about hunting, but closed it when I saw the look on Dad's face. "Please," he said. "Not yet. I need time."

Nana looked pointedly from dad to me. "It's Wylde's choice. It's not yours."

"Wylde," Dad repeated. He rubbed at his neck, then carefully cleared his throat. "Of course. I'm sorry. All of you, really. For everything. It was Wythe. I was trying to do something good. But he – no. I'm sorry. After all this time, I should have known—"

"No one listened," Kai said softly. "I tried to tell you."

Dad turned toward Kai, shaking his head. "I know," he said, his mouth a hard line. "I know. I just wanted..." His words faded, and he wiped his hand slowly across his forehead. He finally looked at me. *Really* looked at me. "Your Mom. She was sick. And I thought I could...I tried to...but I couldn't." He stared down at his hands, like they weren't strong enough. Like if he could just fix them, he could have fixed everything.

"You didn't," I said.

Kai shook his head. "Adults are so immature sometimes."

Nana laughed. "They really are. But it's gonna be okay. We'll get it worked out."

"We will," Dad said, turning back to me. "I'm so sorry."

I clenched and unclenched my fist, then shoved it back into my pocket again. My skin was sizzling. "We have a lot to talk about."

"We do," Dad said.

Nana clicked her tongue. "There'll be time for that. But we need to get that hand looked at first." I started, and Nana raised an eyebrow. "You think I didn't notice that pile of chunky curry?"

"Curry is yellow," I said. She put her hand on her hip, and I took a deep breath. "Back to Dr. Mamau?"

"Yes." She looked down at Kai. "And you're coming too. Those wings. I've seen them before. I had almost forgotten..." She stared down at them, her face unreadable. "So many stories colliding."

Jules raised her hand – just like we were back at school – then smacked me with her wing. "Sorry," she said. "They don't work right yet."

Nana pointed at me, Jules and Kai. "You three need to practice. We'll meet you at the hospital."

Jaiden shuffled his feet, and I caught his eye again. "Seriously," I said. "I'm sorry. Maybe we can get you some later?"

"It's cool. Don't worry. I'll be fine."

"He'll be great," Nana said. "Like a chicken in a blanket."

"That's not a thing," Jaiden said. Nana glared at him, but he just laughed. "It's not!"

She shooed him away and called for DD.

"Where's Brad?" I asked.

"Supply closet," Nana said.

"You going to let him out?"

"Maybe. We should fix that tynged."

"What's a tynged?" Jaiden asked.

"It makes him dumb," I said.

"You mean his brain?" Jaiden asked.

"Exactly," Nana said. "I'll ask the Afanc. Brad must have made someone incredibly mad. The tynged is unbelievably strong. Someone doesn't want him to remember."

"There wasn't a lot to forget," Jaiden said. "He was already pretty dumb."

DD bounded up to Nana and she rubbed behind his ears. "He's coming with us."

Jaiden shivered. "In the car?"

Nana smiled. "It's not a car."

Jaiden sighed, and I reached over and patted DD's head. He sniffed my blue hand, then licked me hesitantly. It felt, well, really wet and gross.

I wiped the slobber on my pants and glanced over at Dad. "See you there?"

"I'll wait for the police. Make sure everything goes okay. Call me when you get there."

"Will do."

"Really."

"I will."

"Stay safe."

"I'll try."

Mom,

If you're there, thanks. You were right. You always were. Everything is just like you said.

I have wings. Seriously! It's still really weird, but I think you'd love them. All that magic makes me feel like I'm all filled up with something. Possibility? Hope? Maybe. I'm starting to think that things could get better.

Plus, I think Dad is on his way back. At least, I hope so. There's these moments when I see him back in there, somewhere. I thought I lost you both. I can't do that again.

I miss you so much,

Wylde

31

We stood on the roof, looking down over the city. The sun was rising. Kai was already slicing through the air, his giant dragon wings cutting the clouds in half.

Jules swallowed hard. I heard that little click in her throat. "You really did this?" she said.

I looked out into the sunrise. "I didn't have to think about it. The light slammed me through a window. I just kind of fell."

"And then you flew."

"I raised my arms like this." My wings spread out behind me. "Eventually, your wings will work on their own. Mine do sometimes, but not all the time. So, I move my arms, and the wings move with them. Try it."

She stretched out her wings. Her feathers pulled through her torn shirt. Maple brown and white with a hint of gold at the tips. They flashed behind her red hair. Breathtaking.

"I don't think I can do it, Wylde. I'm not you."

I nodded, wondering who she thought I was. I don't think I would do that either. "You totally don't have to. We can do this another way, I think. Try this." I flapped my arms, wings beating the air. I rose off the ground.

She shook out her hands, then raised them to the sky and beat them back down. Her feet left the shingles.

A magnificent smile flooded her face. "I did it! I'm doing it!" She rose up into the sky, and rays of morning sunlight splashing gold as she jerked into the air. "Let's do this!" she said.

Then she dove off the side, a scream of joy on her lips.

I dove down after her, spreading my wings wide.

And we flew.

The End

ACKNOWLEDGMENTS

Kate and Brian are endlessly lucky to have the love of their amazing families and the care of their Oregon writing communities. This novel came to life because of Kate and Brian's belief in the possibility of hope and wonder, and the book is in your hands because of the incredible support of our Kickstarter. We could not have done it without these 100 backers!

Peter & Carter Neuleib, Alex & Jillian Purdie, Matthew Bird, Debby Dodds, Gigi Little, Daryll Lynne Evans, Fiona Mackintosh, The Creative Fund, Katherine Lodge, Lisa Elliott, Jamie L Nelson, Valerie Sasaki, Jeanine Sawyer, Katie Fouks, Maren Anderson, Danielle Dumont & Joel Michael, Douglas Chase, Charlie Nash, Russell Nohelty, Jeanne Anderson, Nichole Davis, Jim Harris, Annie Carl, Kristin Noreen, Daniel Lago, Benjamin Gorman, Stephanie Edwards, Tim, Curtis C. Chen, Dan Berne, Don Presten, Jennifer, Jill Johnson, Toinette Thomas, Daniel Porter, Kim DeForest, Cary McGehee, Jess J. Patton, Louette Kleffner, Joe Jatcko, Yvonne Gauntt, Katrinka Mannelly, Kristi Holsinger, Robert Monge, Susan Hill Long, Wayne Anderson, Irina Shields, Alison Jakel, Kevin Rice, Nora Putterman, Jenny Gamboa, Ansley Flores, Tiffany Dickinson,

Michele Ray, Mary Meredith Drew, Joe Nelson, Crystal & Tom Anderson, Tony Salm, Christine Hanolsy, Wendy Wallace, Barbara Parker-Sanders, Elisa Saphier, Rosalyn & Magic & Rowan Ristau, Halsted M. Bernard, Josh Anderson, Meredith Cook, Katie Warren, Dorinne, Bridget Bayer, Margaret Kavanaugh, Laura Stanfill, Nikee Holabird, Elizabeth Philippi, Erik Grove, Corey Mackura, Jenny Forrester, Unchaste Readers Series, Tina Yep, Brandon Simchuk, Karen Eisenbrey, Nancy Ballard, Michael Deneweth, Remy Nakamura, Grant Riddell, Grace Julian, Michelle Carlson, Jennifer Lindsay, Debra Moffitt, Stephanie Bates, Jaym Gates, KC Cowan, Masako Sakurada Castile, Grace Hansen, Jaclyn Simchuk, Simone Cooper, Nancy, James Kleffner, Eric T. Sorlien, Tamiko K. Little, and Kathleen Colvin.

Your love is Wylde, my friends. Thank you.

ABOUT THE AUTHOR

Kate Ristau is a folklorist and the author of the middle grade series, *Clockbreakers*, and the young adult series, *Shadow Girl*. She is the Executive Director of Willamette Writers, a nonprofit organization for writers. You can read her essays in *The New York Times* and *The Washington Post*. In her ideal world, magic and myth combine to create memorable stories with unforgettable characters. Until she finds that world, she'll live in a house in Oregon, where they found a sword behind the water heater and fairies in the backyard. Find out more about Kate at Kateristau.com.

ABOUT THE ILLUSTRATOR

Brian W. Parker grew up in Alaska, then Mississippi, and has always been in love with storytelling in every medium. He earned a BFA in graphic design & illustration and an MA in writing & publishing, and now spends his days working in youth publishing through his own publishing company, Believe In Wonder, which he co-owns with his wife. He is the author of *Crow in the Hollow, You Can Rely on Platypi*, and *The Wondrous Science*. Find out more about Brian at Believeinwonder. weebly.com/

A NOTE ABOUT THE TEXT

Did you notice words that weren't English in this book? Awesome! We didn't italicize them for a reason – we think it makes English look better or more important than other languages when you put it in italics.

That's not cool.

Want to know more? You can read the article by Khairani Barokka in *Catapult Magazine* called "The Case Against Italicizing 'Foreign' Words."

Good work paying attention, my friend!

The novel pages of this book are presented in Meridian font. The illustrated pages primarily use Hidalgo font, along with Ocean and Noteworthy.

Did you know graphic designers and artists created these fonts? We love their work and hope you do too!

CPSIA information can be obtained
at www.ICGtesting.com
Printed in the USA
LVHW080802141121
703215LV00001B/5